Mrs Compton Reade

Rose and Rue

A Novel: Vol. I.

Mrs Compton Reade

Rose and Rue
A Novel: Vol. I.

ISBN/EAN: 9783337031992

Printed in Europe, USA, Canada, Australia, Japan

Cover: Foto ©Andreas Hilbeck / pixelio.de

More available books at **www.hansebooks.com**

ROSE AND RUE.

A Novel.

BY

MRS. COMPTON READE.

" She was a maiden of most quiet face,
  Tender of speech, and had no hardihood,
  But was nigh feeble of her fearful blood ;
  Her mercy in her was so marvellous."

  . . . .
  SWINBURNE'S "ST. DOROTHY."

To me every hour of the light and dark is a miracle,
Every inch of space is a miracle,
Every square yard of the surface of the earth is spread with the same,
Every cubic foot of the interior swarms with the same ;
Every spear of grass, the frames, limbs, organs of men and women, and all
    that concerns them,
All these to me are unspeakably perfect miracles."
  WALT WHITMAN'S " MIRACLES.'

IN THREE VOLUMES.

VOL. I.

LONDON:

RICHARD BENTLEY AND SON.

1874.

TO

JAMES HENDERSON, ESQ.,

E Dedicate

THIS BOOK,

IN TOKEN OF MY SINCERE GRATITUDE

FOR ENCOURAGEMENT AND ASSISTANCE

AS GENEROUSLY AND KINDLY

AFFORDED,

AS HEARTILY APPRECIATED.

CONTENTS OF VOL. 1.

ROSE AND RUE.

CHAPTER I.

THE DARKNESS THAT MAKETH AFRAID.

"HARK!" exclaimed Tryphena Fowke, one Saturday evening in September, 1821, the year that George the Fourth was crowned, that Napoleon died —"what was that?"

"It sounded like a gun being fired," replied the person appealed to, a middle-aged woman of staid, and even severe aspect, who was engaged in stoning damsons at a table near the window—the creeper-framed lattice window of the kitchen at Shobdon Grange.

"But it is too late for any one to be out shooting now!" argued Tryphena, glancing at

the eight-day clock which stood in the corner
by the door—a solemn, white-faced clock, surmounted by a skeleton in the act of mowing ;
"I can scarcely see to work."

"The nights do draw in, I grant!" answered the severe-looking woman, with re-
luctance, as if she felt personally aggrieved
thereby ; "you'd better get a light."

"No, thank you," said the girl, meekly, re-
threading her darning needle with patient
assiduity. "I dare say I shall be able to
finish these stockings! Father would call it
waste to have candles burning at half-past
seven!"

"Your father knows the cost of things!"
returned the severe-looking woman, severely.
"He has to pay for them!"

To this remark Tryphena vouchsafed no
answer. Indeed, no answer seemed to be re-
quired ; moreover, such energies as she had
at her command were centred in the act of
vision. Wherefore, her companion being
little given to superfluous speech, they re-
lapsed into silence, and the old clock, the
smouldering, cracking logs on the hearth,
and the asthmatic pointer stretched before

it, resumed that undisturbed communion
which they had enjoyed previous to the
utterance of the exclamation which heads
this chapter.

There are few places better loved by
shadows, I find, than a farm-house kitchen
—an old farm-house kitchen that is; one
cannot well connect obscurity with the spic-
and-span propriety and even elegance of those
newer structures wherein our wealthy agri-
culturists elect to dwell amongst their flocks
and herds. The ghost must indeed be hard
to lay, and devoid of sensibility, who should
presume to haunt farm-buildings constructed
after plans which have taken prizes at International Exhibitions, and tenanted by kine
worth from fifty to twelve hundred guineas a
head and the latest improvements in every
kind of implement; but at the time of which
I am now writing International Exhibitions
and show yearlings were equally unknown.
The farmer who should have mooted the
notion of a steam plough in the bar or coffee-
room of the inn whither he resorted on
market days for refreshment and the agreeable interchange of sentiment after the wear

and tear of business, would have run the risk
of forfeiting his reputation for sanity, and a
safe taste in politics from that day forward;
might even have found himself classed with
those deluded and wrong-headed persons who
desired the emancipation of Catholics, and
looked back on the Peterloo demonstration
with feelings other than regretful. Men
thought as their fathers, lived as their fathers,
died as their fathers. To fear God, honour
the king, distrust Mr. O'Connell, and hate
the French, constituted the national *codex
simplex* of virtues. The Briton who built his
convictions on these foundations laboured well
and to good purpose. Those who came after
him would not be left shelterless. He might,
if he were so disposed, add one or two supple-
mentary clauses—such as " spare the rod and
spoil the child ;" " wilful waste makes woful
want ;" " each for himself, and God for us
all ;" but this was scarcely necessary, seeing
he would be certain to find these wholesome
views well developed and actively enforced in
whatever rank of life Providence, aided by
his parents, might have placed him. No,
elaboration was mere waste of time, and more-

over savoured of Jesuitism and new-fangled-
ness. That a man must have principles no
one could deny ; but those principles should
be sound, and the closer in accordance with
the family teaching the better. Thus, Shob-
don-cum-Shackerley, being one of the sleepiest,
peacefullest villages to be found even in the
sleepy, peaceful west ; a fruitful, hill-sheltered,
tree-fanned, rose-wreathed morsel of a place,
with but two respectable-sized houses within its
borders—one, the vicarage, now vacant, owing
to the recent death of the vicar, and the other
this Shobdon Grange, whither you have
already penetrated ; and Farmer Fowke, the
proprietor of this last-named tenement by
right of heritage, continued through long
generations, being Conservative by inclination, as well as a sense of fitness—it is
scarcely to be wondered at that innovation
hesitated to cross his threshold, and that
the shadows held high revel in his kitchen, as
being old and brown and full of memories,
and in every way the very place for shadows
to hold high revel in.

But even shadows may not boast complete
exemption from those natural restrictions

which so cramp and fetter this our poor
humanity. By the time the leisurely and
dogged clock from whose interior proceeded
every now and then creaks and groans, not
unlike the disconnected grumbling of some
rheumatic veteran who feels past work and
yet will labour on while life remains; by the
time this leisurely and dogged clock, I say,
had ticked away another ten minutes of the
gray, reposeful evening — gray with wide-
spreading clouds, reposeful with the sense
of labour ended—the light had so faded that
Tryphena found it impossible to go on with
her work, and rose to light the candles standing on the ample, well-furnished dresser,
which ran along one side of the kitchen.

"You'll find some spills by your father's
snuff-box," said the severe-looking woman,
wiping her hands on her apron, having just
stoned the last damson; "I put 'em there
myself when I was doing down the shelves
this morning."

"Yes; here they are," responded Tryphena.
"Shall I light one candle or both?"

"One. I must make up the fire, if I'm
to give these plums their first scald to-night.

There! get out of the way, dog. It's time you were destroyed, I think ; you're no good to yourself or anybody else."

" Poor old Beauty !" smiled Tryphena, patting the pointer's head, " you've been a good dog in your day ; it would be a shame not to let you take your own time about dying, wouldn't it ?"

" There's some one at the door !" exclaimed the elder woman, throwing a couple of logs on the fire, which sputtered and crackled its acknowledgment of the favour ; " go and see who it is."

" It's one of the men, most likely," replied Tryphena, placing the candle now lit on the table by her work-basket ; " or Tapp."

" Tapp's no business here at this time of night !" responded the other tartly ; " he should be in the fold-yard seeing to the calves."

" Deed, 'm !" exclaimed a voice from the gloom.

It was that of a roughly-dressed, weather-beaten-looking man, who had lifted the latch and entered while she was speaking, a man whose prevailing tint from the crown of his

round large head to the soles of his huge
thick boots was that of rust ; even his face—
not quite unprepossessing, despite its flat nose,
wide mouth, and ragged fringe of reddish
whisker—even his face and hands, by reason
of multitudinous freckles, partaking of the
local colour.

"Deed, 'm ! and what if I 'ave been in the
fold-yard, and 'ave seen to the calves ?"

"In that case you would have done your
duty," responded the severe-looking woman
coldly.

"Yes," answered he, dryly—"yes ; I should
'a done my duty—I should 'a done my duty ;
and "—with a slow smile, showing rusty teeth,
large irregular teeth, teeth which scarcely
added to the charm of his appearance—
"that's what John Tapp mostly does do, I
think, though folks seem slow to see it. But
I ain't come to argyfy. Mebbe you 'erd a
gun go off some quarter of a hour ago ?"

"Yes," replied Tryphena, reseating herself
at the table, and putting on her thimble ; "and
we were surprised, because it was too dark,
we thought, for any one to be out shooting."

"That 'ud depend on the kind o' game 'e

was arter," grinned Tapp. "Some game's easiest got late!"

"What do you mean?" inquired the elder woman. "Has the master been murdered?"

"The maister's not been murdered," answered Tapp, with significant deliberation; "but some one else 'as, or thereabouts."

"Gracious!" ejaculated Tryphena, turning as white as the tucker in her dress, a flowered chintz with a chocolate ground, "where? How?"

"Well, 'ow ain't so easy to say," was the leisurely answer; "but weer's soon told. I found un under the 'edge in Goose Lane."

"Bless me!" exclaimed the girl, clasping her hands with horror, "how terrible! Whatever ought we to do? Aunt Rachel, what is to be done?"

"Hold your tongue, child!" commanded Aunt Rachel, "and let me get at the rights of it. Is the man dead or alive?"

"'E ain't much alive!" responded Tapp, slowly, considering his hat.

"But is he dead?"

"Well, no, I don't think 'e's that, unless 'e's died since I left un."

"Where is he!"

"Weer 'e was when I found un. Coorse, 'tweern't no use a-draggin' of un 'ere, till I'd seen whether you'd take un in."

"But you didn't leave him alone?"

"No. I left Tom with un, a-'oldin' the 'orse. I ketched that a-comin' down the lane —that was 'ow I come to find the poor feller."

"Humph—well," and Aunt Rachel paused as if to deliberate,—"I should say you'd better take one of the carts and some one to help you—perhaps Jim Goodwin's not gone home yet—and fetch him up here as quick as you can. I only hope he's not a Papist."

John smiled.

"That 'ud be a rare start for Mr. Latchet," remarked he. "'E could try 'is 'and at convartin' of un!"

"Mr. Latchet would act to the glory of God, whatever circumstances he might be placed in," replied Aunt Rachel, frigidly.

"Perhaps Tom could ride off for Dr. Sprague, while you were bringing the poor man here," interposed Tryphena, who was of a practical and sympathetic turn of mind, and apt to realize the anguish of others with unpleasant clearness.

"P'raps 'e could!" returned Tapp. "I'll see. It's a nasty job, and one I'd as soon not be mixed up in; but I shouldn't like to be left in sech a plight myself—-so"——

"You'd better look sharp, if you mean to do any good," exclaimed Aunt Rachel not without acerbity. "If the man's as bad as you make out, and not drunk, he's bleeding to death while you're standing gabying here. Much use in getting carts, and sending four miles for a doctor, when the poor creature's all but a corpse."

"Lor' bless me!" ejaculated John Tapp, facing round towards the door, "a body need be made o' india-rubber to please you, Miss Rachel;" and therewith took his departure as unceremoniously as he had come.

"Well," said Tryphena, when the garden gate had banged behind him, "this is a pretty business!"

"I see no need for you to make an outcry," responded Aunt Rachel, promptly, going to the hearth and stirring the logs to a brighter flame; "it'll make no difference to you."

"But the idea of his coming in like that— just as if nothing had happened, and telling it as quiet——"

" What would you have had him do ?" was the tart rejoinder—" crack up the furniture, and bawl like a madman ?"

" Dear, no," said Tryphena, quite shocked by the effluence of her aunt's imagination ; " but—— I wish father was at home."

" If wishes were horses beggars would ride. Go upstairs and get me a pair of sheets out of the linen-chest. Stay, here's the key. Mind you give it me back. And a couple of pillow-cases," in a shriller tone, as the girl left the kitchen. " Thieves are no worse than a damp bed."

Quickly sped Tryphena on her errand, down the long stone passage, across the chill large hall, and up the broad oaken stairs, dull and pale from lack of care and beeswax, but of a good pitch, and garnished with massive, deeply-moulded bannisters, which might have well made a London turner jealous. Murder has ever a ghastly sound, be the circumstances thereto attached never so remote from one's personal experience ; but when murder comes close—halts at one's threshold, as it were— surely it is not to be wondered at that this meek maid turned pale, and held her breath fearfully, as she faced the dark corners and mysterious vaguenesses of that quaint old house. It already was possessed of one indubitable ghost—a little old lady dressed in a yellow satin sac, a large black beaver hat, with black feathers, and red, high-heeled shoes, with powdered hair and an ebony walking-cane, who was given to gathering the water-lilies which grew in Poynder's Pond (John Tapp's father saw her there one June night as he came home from Chadlington fair—saw her as plain as ever he saw anybody in his life)— and was suspected of having doings with two more, besides being further gifted with auturgic doors and self-emptying milk-pans :—Tryphena made haste.

But, expeditious as she was, Aunt Rachel lacked not cause for stimulating utterance on her return, being one of those prosperous and happily-constituted persons who are seldom out of grievances.

"Come, come," exclaimed she, as the girl re-entered the kitchen, her arms full of homespun lavender-scented linen, "do move a bit quicker : one would think you'd got the rheumatics, you walk so slow !"

" I was afraid of dropping the grease !" said Tryphena, submissively, depositing her burden on the table.

" Pshaw !" ejaculated Aunt Rachel, stirring the damsons as they simmered on the hob. " Where's the clothes-horse ?"

" In the scullery," replied Tryphena. " I'll go and get it. Which room is he to have ?"

" Mine," was the prompt reply.

" But where will you sleep, then ?"

" Sleep !" echoed Miss Fowke, contemptuously—" sleep indeed ! Much sleep I'm likely to get for the next month to come !"

" Oh, I forgot !" smiled Tryphena, reappearing with the clothes-horse ; " of course he'll require a great deal of attention, poor man, that is if he isn't dead already."

For a while the bustle of preparation upstairs in the scantily furnished and somewhat gloomy chamber wherein Miss Fowke nightly disposed her weary and not unangular limbs to rest ; downstairs, in the spacious, shadow-haunted, fruit-perfumed kitchen, which that strong-minded, far-seeing lady caused to be cleared of all unnecessary articles of furniture, all things likely to fall down of their own evil

will or by the machinations of others, alleging
as a reason for such clearance that when
Tryphena's grandfather broke his collar-bone
the doctor declared that the parts would never
bind if the house wasn't kept quiet, owing to
the nerves—for a while, I repeat, the bustle
consequent on these alterations, which were
effected entirely by the two women themselves
—Farmer Fowke keeping no servant, being of
a saving disposition—rendered conversation
other than monosyllabic something less than
desirable or even possible. But willing arms
make short tasks.

"There!" exclaimed Tryphena, when the
last chair was carried away into the parlour,
and the great horsehair sofa rolled con-
veniently near the kitchen door, in case the
stranger should swoon on being removed from
the cart, "now I think we're ready, and they
may come as quick as they please!"

"They are coming!" answered Aunt Rachel,
pausing, duster in hand, to listen, her keen
hazel eyes fixed on the girl's flushed face—a
sweet oval face, pure as pictured saint's—
"I hear the cart!"

"Yes!" said Tryphena, listening too; "so

do I! Oh, dear!" and she clasped her hands, and turned herself about as if inclined to flee forthwith.

"What's the matter now?" inquired Aunt Rachel, sternly.

"I'm so frightened. I do wish father was at home. Fancy if he dies!"

"Fancy a fiddlestick!" scoffed Aunt Rachel, going to the door. "If you're going to give way to that nonsense, you'd better take yourself off upstairs. I don't want any hysterics down here! I shall have my hands full enough as it is. Who's that?"

"Me, mum!" replied the voice of John Tapp from out the twilight. "I thowt as I'd just step up afore we brought un to the door to see if you weer ready."

"Yes, I'm ready," replied Aunt Rachel. "Where's he hurt?"

"'E says 'e were shot at from be'ind," responded Tapp—"shot at and wounded in the shoulder, and sure enough his ridin'-coat's a-dranched wi' blood; but we'd better get un laid down. I've sent Jim for the doctor."

"That's right," said Aunt Rachel, and set the door wide open to throw what light she could upon the roughly-paved path, bordered with rosemary bushes and thick patches of sweet herbs, up which the stranger must walk or be carried.

"Perhaps he isn't so bad as he thinks," adventured Tryphena, tremulously, peering out with great scared eyes, blue as the wild geraniums fringing her father's meadows; "perhaps he won't die after all."

"You go to bed!" exclaimed Aunt Rachel, with alarming promptitude. "I've told you once before I don't want you down here."

But the girl made no answer, neither did she move; her attention was riveted on that which was taking place before her.

Past the back premises of the Grange, ran a road used only by the farm labourers and such persons as had business at the house. Down this road was now being driven slowly, and with care, a cart, in which sat Tom Tapp, John Tapp's son, and another; John Tapp himself holding open the yard gate, and adjuring Tom to "pull up gentle, so as not to jolt the gentleman."

"Oh, dear!" exclaimed Tryphena, "hadn't I better get the brandy?"

"Yes," replied Aunt Rachel, hastily snatching up a candle, and hurrying out to afford the sufferer the support of her presence during his transit from the cart into the house; "get the brandy and a wineglass, and measure out about a tablespoonful."

A rattle of shaken harness—a low murmur of voices—a clatter of heavily-shod feet—and Typhena turned—the bottle in one hand, the glass in the other—to see a tall fair man in a long gray riding-coat, from which dripped steadily small drops of blood as rain from the eaves of a thatched house, stagger weakly through the door, supported by Tom Tapp, and fall heavily upon the sofa.

A moment or two of paralyzing horror, and she hurried towards him, stricken with pity for his most pitiable condition.

"Drink this, sir," said she, holding out the glass; "it will do you good. John, do get him to take it!"

But John shook his head. The man had fainted.

CHAPTER II.

SUNDAY dawned chill and sunless—the clouds of the preceding evening still hung darkly overhead, though the moistened roads and spangled greenery showed that it had already rained during the night. Tryphena Fowke shivered when, on rising, she looked out of her little, old-fashioned, white-draped window upon the prim flower garden, with its pyramidal box trees clipped and carved into the semblance of dumb-waiters, its fading asters, its shabby geraniums, its dishevelled dahlias, and sturdy marigolds. The world seemed so full of death.

Turning from the imaginative and exterior to the practical and interior aspect of things, however, the world could scarcely be held so

2—2

funereal as it might have been. For instance, the stranger upon whom Aunt Rachel kept constant and untiring watch, suffering no interference, even to the harmless extent of making inquiries, might have expired from loss of blood or anguish beneath Dr. Sprague's probe and lancet, or have turned feverish at the least; whereas he had not only endured the extraction of the bullet, which had lodged under his left shoulder-blade, with extraordinary fortitude and composure, but had actually seemed better afterwards, and inclined for sleep—sleep, which the doctor said was more likely to remove the evil effects of exhaustion, and initiate a satisfactory convalescence, than all the drugs in the king's physician's medicine chest—excepting, of course, calomel, rhubarb, colocynth, and, for occasional use, jalap.

Still Tryphena shivered as she looked out of her window that first-day morning—shivered and yawned; there had been so much wet of late.

On passing Aunt Rachel's door, as the old clock struck six—folks were astir early in Shobdon Grange—she paused and listened; some one was moving.

" Aunt !" said she, almost in a whisper, and gave a gentle little tap.

Promptly that lady made her appearance, attired in a red moreen petticoat, a chintz bedgown, and a voluminous nightcap—to sleep, to even doze, in one's day-clothes being an enormity not to be contemplated without shrinking by a person of sober and industrious habits, with a fine sense of duty and the danger of the unregenerate.

" Well !" replied she ; " what do you want ?"

" How is he ?"

" He is asleep."

" Does he seem in great pain ?"

" No ; he groans now and then, and frowns, but that's only what must be expected !"

" Would you like me to sit with him a bit, while you dress or lie down ?"

" No !" responded Aunt Rachel, severely ; " most certainly not. I wonder at your thinking of such a thing—a young girl like you. If I want to put on my gown, I can do so without your help. The idea of such forwardness !"

" But I only meant to be useful," responded

Tryphena, aggrievedly; "you do take things so;" and the tears twinkled in her eyes.

Miss Fowke's expression waxed ironical.

"That's right," smiled she—"cry away; it'll do you good."

"You are very unkind," was the indignant answer; "it's all one whether I try to do well or ill, as far as I see. That's not the way to make a person better."

"Go down, and get on with the work," rejoined Aunt Rachel, coolly; "and bring me up some more barley-water. You can set it outside the door; and when Martha Tapp comes, tell her I want her. She'll be here soon."

"Very well," replied Tryphena, drying her eyes with her apron, and forthwith proceeded downstairs; but her tone was not cheerful, neither was her step brisk.

In good sooth, this young woman's life was somewhat bare of pleasantness—somewhat bleak and wind-scourged, as waste land in a hilly region.

"It is like Wynn Common," thought she, one day, when driven by lack of pleasanter matter for reflection to self-analysis, "and my soul is like the little may-bush by the pond—

a stunted, ugly, lonely little thing, which never opens a bud till all the rest of its brothers and sisters are white with blossom, and about which the bees never hum or the dragon-flies dance or the children play. A yellowhammer would have made her nest in it last year I think, but the wind scattered the sticks and straw and wool before she could get it finished, and so she was forced to go and lay her eggs elsewhere. Yes, that bush is, without doubt, quite curiously like my soul."

At eighteen this kind of reasoning is apt to produce depression, and an inclination to doubt the perfect working of the Providential system, which is scarcely calculated to lessen the evil it suggests. Tryphena Fowke rose early, and went to bed long after she was tired, and did zealously whatever her hands found to do from morning to night, and loved her father, and tried hard to please her aunt, and said her prayers for hours at a time with a fervour and constancy which sometimes struck her as strangely out of keeping with results, and was generally considered in the village and neighbourhood as a fine example of the force of Christian precept and virtuous precedent, combined with early training and sedulous attention to domestic duties. But her face was very grave for a girl, despite its undeniable prettiness and softness of tint, and grew graver month by month ; and her manner was strangely sedate and feelingless—what John Tapp called "'ooden." There were persons who fancied she might have been less unlike other young people if her mother had lived.

However, things were as they were ; the Lord had seen fit to take young Mrs. Fowke to Himself at the early age of twenty-four— just sixteen years ago come next Christmas. She died on Christmas Eve, as the bells began to ring ; and the Lord knew best—little good ever came of guessing.

Sunday was a very quiet day at the Grange, the Fowkes being Methodists by conversion, and keen to discriminate between things temporal and spiritual. Even the dumb creatures, furred and feathered, who dwelt upon the farm, seemed, Aunt Rachel said, to know that they obtained their daily sustenance by God's mercy, through the medium of Christian proprietors—the fowls maintaining a decent gravity of demeanour at feeding-time on the Sabbath, and the dogs a becoming languor and disinclination to venture out of bounds.

By seven o'clock Tryphena, who was too often heavy at heart to let her private annoyances weaken her power of usefulness, had lit the kitchen fire, set on the kettle, set out the breakfast—a plain, scarcely-inviting meal, composed of stale bread, treacle, and milk and water, or porridge, as a person might prefer —swept the kitchen, tidied the dresser, and was free to busy herself with the preparation of that barley-water Aunt Rachel had requested her to make, or satisfy the claims of appetite, according to her liking. Being zealous in the tutelage of self, and not hungry, she, having opened the Bible, which lay ready for use on the kitchen table, and selected a text whereon to meditate during the day as occasion offered, which text ran as follows : " For there is nothing hid which shall not be manifested, neither was anything kept secret but that it should come abroad "— betook herself to the larder, which, in common with the washhouse, was built out from the house among the rosemary bushes and

sweet herbs, in search of the pearl barley and
lemons which had been carried there last night
after the first brew was decocted. As she
returned she glanced down the road, and perceived that a woman had just turned the
corner and was walking quickly towards the
gate.

"Here's Martha, Beauty!" exclaimed she,
as the old dog pricked up her ears. "Good
Martha—you needn't bark at her!"

And Beauty got up slowly—she was stiff
after her long night on the bare stones—and
wagged her tail as if she recognized the justice
of that saying.

On came the woman, on through the gate
up the roughly-paved garden path.

"Good-morning, Martha," said Tryphena,
smiling brightly as she went to the door to
welcome her; "aunt said that you would be
coming."

"Yes, fayther told me last night that I
should be wanted, so I thought I'd just step
up," she answered, following Tryphena to the
fireplace as one who knew her way. "It do
look likely for wet."

"Yes," replied Tryphena, filling a saucepan

with boiling water, "it is always wet now,
I have quite given up hoping for a fine day."

" 'Tain't much use frettin' about the
weather," observed Martha, calmly, taking off
her great purple sun-bonnet and dark shawl,
and hanging them up on a nail driven into the
wall ; " pertickler now that the corn's got in."

A shrewd, sensible, stout-built young
woman was Martha Tapp, with a broad good-
tempered face, freckled like her father's, and
moreover, like his, lit up with keen, small,
red-brown eyes, and framed by coarse rust-
coloured hair, but in other respects better
favoured, notably in the matters of mouth and
teeth—a shrewd, sensible young woman, and
one not inclined to cheapen her own wares.

" What are you doin'?" pursued she, coming
back to the hearth—" makin' porridge ?"

" No," said Tryphena, ladling the barley
into the saucepan ; " barley-water for this
poor man who has so nearly been murdered."

" Ay !" ejaculated Martha, " 'e ought to be
worth sommat, seein' the narrowness of 'is
escape. But you shouldn't do that in a pot,
you should 'ave a jug."

" Should I ?" said Tryphena, for whom

Martha's remarks had ever possessed a certain superiority of ring since the days when they used to make daisy chains and buttercup crowns together, and hunt for lords and ladies, and catch the little brown and green grasshoppers of fine afternoons,—the days when she, Tryphena, was a wee, toddling, yellow-headed creature—her hair darkened as she grew up—and Martha a sturdy-limbed, apple-cheeked hoyden, just in her teens, for there was some eight or nine years of difference in their ages.

"Certainly you should !" was the emphatic answer, accompanied by a revolution in the direction of the dresser, and a clutch at a fit receptacle.

"There !" setting it on the table with a bump, "that's more like the sort of thing. You'd better let me see to it."

"Very well," said Tryphena, moving aside, and casting a glance at her untouched breakfast; "only aunt said· you were to go up to her when you came."

"I'll take this up with me," responded Martha, setting about her work briskly, with fine confidence—the confidence of one who had kept her father's home, being motherless, with success, to the general satisfaction for the last ten years. "I suppose she wants me to 'elp 'er nurse 'im."

"I don't know," answered Tryphena, sitting down and cutting a piece of bread; "she was quite cross when I offered to take her place for a while."

"That may be," allowed Martha, halving a lemon, "that's nat'ral enough."

"Well, but," said Tryphena, argumentatively, pouring some milk into her mug, "we're all women. What's proper for one is proper for all."

"No," answered Martha; "you're mistaken there, Miss Phenie. I don't 'old with you, there, not for one second!"

"Well!" exclaimed Tryphena, after a pause, during which she had come to her second slice—talking made her hungry—"at all events, there was no need to be cross about it, was there?"

"Folks 'as their ways," rejoined Martha, mildly; "and you can't alter 'em."

"But the Bible says, 'Blessed are the meek,'" pursued Tryphena, who, like all

sweet-tempered persons, was endowed with
a very respectable allowance of obstinacy,
"and we all want to be blessed, or we ought
to."

"Blessin's like cursin'," answered Martha,
"just a matter of favour. There's some—it
don't seem to signify what they does—everything goes right with 'em, and there's others
as can never get so much as a pertater to come
up when it's wanted. I've seen a plenty o' that
in my time!"

"God chastens His beloved," said Tryphena, gravely. Sometimes she would be
smitten by a doubt concerning the accuracy
of Martha's mental vision on these points,
points which certainly presented some small
hindrance to that gradual equalization and
absorption of roughnesses, on which so indubi-
tably depends the interior peace and comfort
of the soul; but then the excellence of her
friend's practice would recur to her mind, and
for a while reduce such anxiety to the level of
mere hole-picking and censoriousness—for a
while—until some too truistic utterance should
again abrade faith. "God chastens His beloved," said this scrupulous young person;

"besides, it is not wise to look only at the outside of things."

"Nay," replied Martha, a little sadly, drawing a long breath; "thet's very true. If my poor Will could but ha' seen through all them theer red coats and flags and marchins and trumpetins to the battle-field, weer 'e weer to lose first 'is two legs and then 'is life, a-fightin' for what didn't consarn 'im no more nor it does me— Emp'rers and Dooks, and sich nonsense—I might 'ave 'ad a 'ome of my own by now, and a somethin' to look forward to, instead of draggin' on like this with my 'ead always turned over my shoulder, as you may say, a-tryin' to see that which death alone can show me."

"Poor Martha! dear Martha!" exclaimed Tryphena, most compassionately; "but time will make it better, and--prayer. Remember the road to heaven is easiest found upon one's knees."

"Yes, leastways the minister says so," answered Martha, scarcely as though she felt that fact to be pregnant with the liveliest satisfaction; "but your aunt'll be fine and mad with me standin' 'ere jabberin' while she wants that barley-water.   You don't seem to make much count of it all."

"Make much count of what?" questioned Tryphena, absently, liberating a fly from the treacle-jar.

"Why, of all thet 'appened last night, of this poor fellow upstairs.   I'll bet now you don't know whether 'is 'air's brown or gray?"

"You've lost your wager," smiled Tryphena, placidly, "for it's neither; it's yellow."

Martha laughed.

"Is 'e 'andsome?" asked she, possessing herself of the jug.   "Father said 'e were a strapper, and bold, too, with a nice free way —quite a gentleman."

"I know very little about him," responded Tryphena, rising from her chair, and throwing a bit of bread to Beauty, "except that he fainted the instant he got inside the house, and seemed very heavy to carry upstairs."

"And you ain't a bit curious?"

"Curious!" echoed the girl, almost contemptuously, "what is there to be curious about?   Highway robberies are common enough, surely."

"I weern't speakin' of the robbery,"

replied Martha, "nor yet the robber;" and
then she picked up her gown under her arms
and went upstairs.

Enough idle chatter for one Sabbath morning.

CHAPTER III.

EFT to herself, Tryphena would gladly have resumed that meditative calm which long years of patient struggling against inherent imperfections—imperfections Aunt Rachel ascribed to the accident of her brother Jacob's marriage with a young woman who was known to none of the family, and had always lived in a town —had led her to regard as the fittest mental attitude of one who, being earnestly desirous of increased spiritual experience, should still care to preserve a nice appreciation of relative duties. But strive as she might to fix her attention on things unseen—to surround herself with a luminous atmosphere of holy thought —carnal imaginations, worldly anxieties, rebelliously darkened and defiled her mind.

What was going on upstairs? Was the man worse?—was he awake?—what would he have for his dinner? The family meal would be composed of a leg of pork, turnips, and an apple pudding; but that was scarcely fare suited to the digestive capacities of an invalid. What would he have then, and would they attend service that afternoon, or would Aunt Rachel think it more in accordance with circumstances to stay away, and so give weakly souls no occasion for wandering looks and light whisperings? The elaboration of this hypothesis caused a sigh to escape the girl's red lips, for she found much sustainment during her interior trials in the memory of these hebdomadal gatherings together of the faithful, conducted with great zeal and ability by the Reverend Acts Latchet, the Wesleyan minister at Coatham, in the great barn, every Sunday afternoon during the autumn and winter, and on Sunday evenings in summer.

Rapt in these considerations, despite an occasional effort at disentanglement and the mental repetition of verses from hymns and the Sermon on the Mount, Tryphena flitted to and fro from farm-yard to store-room, from

store-room to larder, from larder to scullery,
scattering grain, measuring flour, peeling potatoes — doing the hundred and one things
which must be done before she could reckon
herself free to get on her Sunday frock—a
plain, brown gingham, of soberer cut and
skimpier dimensions than her other dresses—
without much thought as to how time went,
or the requirements of others.

Thus when Aunt Rachel suddenly made her
appearance, and demanded, with her wonted
lack of hollow ceremony, "whether she hadn't
heard her shouting at the top of the stairs
for the last ten minutes?" she started and
trembled, so that you would have imagined
her employed in nothing less guilty than the
breaking open of the missionary pence box,
or the perusal of, shall we say "Kenilworth,"
which was a new novel then, having been
published at the commencement of the year,
instead of the manufacture of pudding paste.

"Well!" pursued Miss Fowke, surprised
at her confusion—"there's nothing to be so
frightened at, is there? I only asked you a
simple question—one would think I'd pro-
mised you a horsewhipping."

"I didn't hear you coming," explained
Tryphena, smiling at her own nervousness ;
"I was so taken up with one thing and an-
other."

"And never a ha'porth of good among the
lot of 'em, I'll warrant," responded Aunt
Rachel, sourly. "I wonder where my jelly
bag's got to," opening and shutting the dresser
drawers with vigour and rapidity.

"It's in the cupboard on the second shelf."

"Who put it there, I should like to know ?"
demanded Miss Fowke, pulling it out, and
holding it up to the light ; "such senseless
ways !"

"Are you going to make him some jelly ?"
inquired Tryphena, placidly investing the
pudding with its cloth.

"Yes. The doctor said he was to have it,
and he seems to fancy it ; so as I happen to
have those pair of calves' feet in the house—
by the way you can go and get 'em when
you've finished what you're about—I may as
well make a mould and have done with it ;
not that I approve of such messing on the
Lord's day, or would lend my hand to it, if it
wasn't a case of necessity."

"Is he so very ill, then?"

"He's about as bad as he can be. There, do be quick. One would think you expected the pot to blow up in your face, you touch it so gingerly."

"I don't care to dirty my hands more than I need," returned Tryphena with mild composure. "But I thought you said he was asleep?"

"So he was, five hours ago,—how them bells do jangle, jangle, to be sure,—but six o'clock ain't eleven, nor then, now."

"I suppose Dr. Sprague will call this morning?"

"I suppose he will. If not, I must send Tapp with the gig to fetch him. We can't let the man die for the sake of a turnpike toll."

"No," assented Tryphena gravely. "No—that is very certain. Do you think they took his purse?"

"I don't know. He's got his watch and seals all right, and very handsome they are too—worth a good bit of money, I should say. His clothes, too, are almost new."

"Should you fancy he was a gentleman?"

"Yes," replied Aunt Rachel, "I should.
—Yes," she reiterated, after a pause, "he's
got quite that look. But there—what does
that matter, when the corn's ripe and the
reaper is ready, and the Master says 'Thrust
in the sickle?' Naked we come into this
world, and naked we must go out again,
be we gentle or simple. Kings and beggars
stand together before the mercy-seat of
Christ."

Tryphena sighed.

"Shall you go to meeting?" she asked
presently, staring into the fire.

"No," answered Aunt Rachel, "I shall
have too much to do indoors; besides, it might
set the people talking, and after all one does
well not to get over-fond of forms; they only
clog the spirit, and tempt us to set man above
his Maker. You can go if you like."

"Nay," replied Tryphena, shaking her
head, "what you think dangerous, must be
quite hurtful for me; I will stay at home,
too. There is always the Bible."

"Yes," said Aunt Rachel, "there is always
the Bible; not but that the heart must indeed be stony and the mind dull which fails

to get both counsel and consolation from the minister's discourses. Few places are so blessed in their pastor as Shobdon."

Tryphena held her peace ; her opinion on that point being too well known to require repetition.

" And the calves' feet," she exclaimed at length, looking up, as if suddenly aware of continued existence, "what a memory is mine !"

Aunt Rachel smiled.

"You may well say that," rejoined she, coldly ; "go and get them at once."

Novelty, or rather a sense of strangeness, is an effectual quickener of the current of daily life. It was dinner-time before Tryphena "could look round," she said, adopting the homely phraseology common at the Grange, where meaning seldom waited on expression. And with dinner came Dr. Sprague, red-faced, bottle-nosed, hilarious, as was his wont, being never at a loss, according to his own showing, to make both ends meet ; births and deaths alike affording him excuse for jollity, and the copious absorption of refreshments, fluid and solid. Tryphena was a favourite with this worthy gentleman—as indeed she was with most persons, despite her shyness and objection to unnecessary speech.

" Yes, sir," he would say, when turning over the young women of his acquaintance—an acquaintance mostly dating from the moment of their appearance on this nether sphere—in the company of some appreciative friend possessed of extended views concerning shapes and complexions—" Yes, sir, Fowke's daughter will make up into a fine woman some day —a devilish fine woman- -sir, a woman any man might be proud to call his own. Egad, yes !"

And as to be fine and the property of a man was, in the doctor's opinion, the loftiest flight permissible or possible to female ambition, it will be perceived that this saying carried weight.

But to-day he seemed rather inclined to criticize than admire.

" Where's your colour, missie ?" demanded he, on meeting her in the passage on his descent from the sick chamber, Miss Fowke bringing up the rear ; " it's too early for snow yet."

"She does look rather white, to be sure," observed Aunt Rachel thoughtfully. "But it's no wonder, considering the upset we had last night. The autumn, too, generally makes a difference with her, I find; it does with a many girls."

"Yes," said Dr. Sprague, caressing his chin —"yes! Nature is wonderfully universal. Perhaps I had better send her a tonic—just a little something to improve the appetite and strengthen the nerves, you know—steel, bark, camomile."

"Well, perhaps you had," rejoined Aunt Rachel; "not that I am much of a one for dosing myself, except when downright ill. I suppose we shan't see you again till to-morrow?"

"No," replied the doctor; "not unless a change for the worse occurs. At present nothing could be more satisfactory—thanks to your excellent nursing. He may think himself uncommonly lucky to have fallen into such good hands."

"I would rather he hadn't," was the calm rejoinder, "but there it is, and we must do the best we can. I'm afraid Jacob won't like

it, though; men do grumble so at anything
unusual—and of course it will be some time
before he's well again."

"Three weeks at the very least," said Dr.
Sprague; "and perhaps a month. The master
is away?"

"Yes," replied Aunt Rachel; "he started
to go to Chadlington on business—about
some wool—we sheared last week—yesterday
afternoon. I wanted him to put it off till
Monday, because it looked so like rain, and I
do dread his getting wet, being so subject to
erysipelas. But who was I to meddle? Didn't
he know what was good for him as well as
ever I did? So he went, and I don't suppose he'll be back till to-morrow evening."

"Ah, well," ejaculated the doctor, button-
ing up his greatcoat, and walking on towards
the front door, which faced the stairs—"suffi-
cient unto the day is the evil thereof. One
should never regret doing a good action.
Besides, you can't tell how these things will
turn out. This young man may be quite a
distinguished person, and able to render you
some important service in years to come."

Aunt Rachel smiled with the serene confidence of one above the malignities of chance.

"I don't much fancy those kind of romantic surprises ever happen in real life," returned she, composedly; "besides, thank God, we have kept clear of favours hitherto."

"Yes, yes," exclaimed the doctor, deprecatorily, perceiving that he had need of discretion; "to be sure—the idea is absurd. But I was not speaking seriously; I was merely giving utterance to what flashed through my mind at the moment. Goodbye"—putting out his hand—"and mind you don't let him move about too much."

"Oh, but you'll take a glass of wine," interposed Aunt Rachel, feeling in her pocket for her keys, "and a bit of cake. Tryphena, child, run and get a glass and plate."

"No," exclaimed the doctor, laying hold of Tryphena's arm—"no, my dear, pray don't. I must be off at once. Mrs. Cave's little boy has scarlet fever, and it's quite a question whether I shall find him alive—he was so ill yesterday. I came here first because I wouldn't run any risk of infection; but I really must make haste now, so good-bye once more."

"Well," said Aunt Rachel, "of course you know best; but I should like to see you have something all the same. Good-bye. What a nice, cheerful old soul he is, to be sure!" she remarked, as she closed the door, having watched him climb into his gig, pull up the apron, turn the flea-bitten gray Shobdon-wards, and drive away up the road; "and so pleasant in a sick-room!"

"I don't think he would fancy being called old, though," returned Tryphena, mildly; "at least he has a way of looking as if he wouldn't."

"Looking!" echoed Aunt Rachel, sharply —"looking at what?"

"Looking at one!" was the prompt reply.

"Pooh!" ejaculated Aunt Rachel. "Why, the man attended your mother when you were born. Did any one ever hear such rubbish! Go and change your frock, and make yourself decent for dinner. You and your lookings indeed!"

CHAPTER IV.

"WERE I QUIET EARTH THAT WERE NO EVIL."

HE leg of pork trifled with, and the apple pudding done full justice to, specially by Martha Tapp, whose appetite was as robust as her physical development, Tryphena having cleared away the plates and dishes, and fed Beauty on such scraps as she dare appropriate for that purpose (it being held wicked waste at the Grange to bestow a superfluity of aliment on a decrepid and decaying animal), betook herself to the parlour—a gloomy, neutral-tinted, airless apartment, destitute of all ornament, save a pair of hand-screens painted by her mother during her school-days, and mounted on gold sticks, which occupied the high black mantelpiece in company with a

china figure of Father Matthew, and divers samplers and maps, the work of defunct Thirzas and Rebeccas and Rachels, hung picture-wise upon the walls—to read. To read and meditate, as was her custom when debarred by slight illness—she was not very strong—or the untowardness of circumstance, from joining in those weekly devotions where-on she set so great store.

But heartily desirous as she was of making a good use of her solitude, by degrees memory waxed dull and conscience blunt. It had begun to rain, too, and the soft patter of the drops upon the window, driven aslant every now and then by the rising wind, lulled thought as might an opiate.

"It is very cold," said Tryphena to herself, shivering in her skimpy brown gingham dress, and pressing her hands to her pallid cheeks—Dr. Sprague had cause to inquire what she had done with her colour—"and I am very stupid, so stupid that I think I must be going to sleep!" and she turned her face to the drab-coloured wall, and closed her eyes and sighed. In heaven there would be no wet Sundays.

How long she sat there idle, motionless, lost

in dreams—the dreams she liked best, dreams that she would be content to spend her life in if she might—dreams of winged seraphs clad in white, with faces full of God, of the city whereof the light is as a jasper, and the gates are twelve—of Him on whose head are many crowns, and whose eyes are as flames of fire; for this farmer's daughter, this drudge of a meagre household, this victim of meannesses, and vial for the reception of superfluous sourness, was made of the stuff whereof has been fashioned in days gone by a shepherdess of Domremi, by name Jeanne d'Arc, a virgin called Teresa Sanchez, better known as St. Teresa, foundress of the reformed order of barefooted Carmelites; a Marguerite Marie Alacoques—how long this unpractical and visionary young woman sat there lost in dreams, I repeat, she would have been hard set to tell, for the soul takes little account of time. However, the clock was striking five when she opened her eyes, and, what was more, some one was knocking at the front door.

With a start which flushed her face red as the tiny fuchsia bells swaying to and fro outside the window—at Shobdon fuchsias flourished rarely, attaining quite tree-like dimensions—she rose to her feet, and hurried out into the passage.

As she crossed the hall, Aunt Rachel, wearing her second best silk, a steel gray, made with leg-of-mutton sleeves, and a tippet, likewise her best cap, a helmet-like structure, decorated with blue ribbons, rustled sumptously downstairs.

"It'll be the minister!" said she, patting down her ample tambour collar; "I hope the kettle's boiling!"

Tryphena opened the door.

"Ah, how do you do?" exclaimed a short, dark gentleman, attired in lustrous black, who was standing under the porch—a gentleman whose white cravat instantly proclaimed the justice of Miss Fowke's anticipations; "I missed you at service, so I thought I would give you a call on my way home, and satisfy myself of your well-being." This shaking hands.

"And very kind of you too!" remarked Aunt Rachel, coming forward to claim her share of greeting; "but I suppose you have already heard the cause of our absence?"

"No," he answered, assuming an expression of mild curiosity, and rubbing his feet on the mat—"no, I have heard nothing except that Mrs. Beer has had twins again," with a gentle little laugh, which accorded well with the mellow and carefully modulated tone of his voice and the placid amiability of his face—a broad, large-featured, black-whiskered face, indicative at once of uncommon mental power and strong animal instincts, the brow and eyes being remarkably fine, especially the former, which presented towards the temples a quite remarkable amount of development, and the mouth and slightly prognathous jaw, coarse and sensual.

"Dear, dear!" said Aunt Rachel, gravely, leading the way to the parlour; "and with ten children already. What can the people be thinking about?"

Mr. Latchet laughed again, and sought for his handkerchief.

Tryphena made a step towards the kitchen.

"What, going to run away already!" exclaimed he, deprecatorily.

"I must get the tea," she answered. "Aunt will keep you company."

Mr. Latchet put his head on one side and smiled as though he failed to derive complete satisfaction from that assurance. Then he followed Miss Fowke.

Deftly did Tryphena set about the preparation of their evening meal.

It was pleasant to her to wait upon the fleshly weaknesses of this man—even if those weaknesses necessitated the scorching of one's cheeks in the making of toast, and the wetting of one's feet in the seeking for new-laid eggs. He had for the last three years—the old minister died when she was fifteen—constituted the centre and motive power of her liveliest interests ; such small religious knowledge as she possessed was the effect of his assiduous teachings and preachings. If she were saved, it would be through his instrumentality. This she thought not blasphemously, but with a keen though mute appreciation of sympathetic causes. How was it possible, then, that she could mind taking pains on his account ?

She did not.

She made as much haste as ever she could,

4—2

and bumped the parlour door with her tea-tray just as Aunt Rachel concluded the recital of last night's horrors.

"Humph!" ejaculated the minister, tucking his feet under the sofa—"humph! Peculiar, very, and far from comfortable. One doesn't like to think of spots, sweet in themselves, and made still sweeter by memory"—with an upward glance at Tryphena (last Sunday evening she walked with him through Goose Lane as far as Peter's stile), "being soiled with crime."

"I'm only very glad that the rascals didn't attack us," said Aunt Rachel, helping to set forth the plates and knives; "for what could we have done, two lone women left by themselves in this great house?"

"Yes," returned Mr. Latchet, "that was indeed a mercy; but we are never beyond the reach of Divine aid, however inopportune circumstances may appear."

"No," responded Aunt Rachel, straightening the cake dish—"no; but this house stands back a good bit from the road all the same, and Jacob, often as I've begged him not to, will keep money in the plate chest."

"I suppose you were vastly alarmed?" smiled the minister, presently, addressing Tryphena, who was taking a last survey of her labours; "it must have seemed as though you had suddenly entered the region of romance."

"No," she replied, mentally counting the egg-spoons, "it did not happen in the least as it would have in a story. John Tapp just came and told us, and then went to fetch him in the waggon, and Jim went for the doctor, and that was all. I think I've got everything now."

Mr. Latchet laughed, and clasped his hands —large sinewy hands, hirsute and sun-burnt — about his right knee. He had found occasion for mirth in the innocent placidity of this young woman before now.

"I do not approve of nervousness," said Aunt Rachel, "when not caused by ill-health; and I have always endeavoured to check it in Tryphena. Now she has had an opportunity of seeing for herself how right I have been. Will you ask a blessing, sir?"

Thus called upon Mr. Latchet rose to his feet, joined his hands together, closed his eyes for a brief space, and then in a few simple, well-chosen words, prayed for a further outpouring of good gifts, spiritual and temporal, and set forth the gratitude now felt for those already vouchsafed.

"Amen!" said Aunt Rachel, when he had made an end of speaking, and "Amen!" said Tryphena, each fervently, with all their heart.

It was wonderful with what effect this man could stir the minds of his hearers. Instances were on record of his having turned sinners to repentance by one sermon—heinous sinners— and by no moderate conventional means, rather with a sudden wrench and indignant outcry, so that the foul soul could not but recognize her foulness at a glance—had no choice but to be made clean. Nor were these conversions transient. Once fairly awakened, it would not be Acts Latchet's fault if you went to sleep again—that is, if preaching could keep you on the alert. A natural orator, to expand and forcibly announce the Gospel tidings was to him not merely the necessary exercise of a professional function, but a delight. To dwell upon the Divine attributes, to paint the sufferings of Christ, to follow Him hither and thither through the cornfields, and crowded streets, to the seashore, up the green slopes of Olivet, afforded him as keen enjoyment as ever artist found in the use of pen or pencil, as ever speculator derived from the successful over-reaching of a fellow-creature. And yet, fortunate as he had been in his ministry to others, his own spiritual experiences were far from reassuring. When he was a youth, despite grievous conflicts with the power of evil, despite the scoffs and calumnies of a worldly and prelatical society—his parents being ardent believers in the virtues of Establishment and fondly attached to the involuntary system—despite these inequalities in his heavenward path, Acts had reason to believe himself predestined to salvation, partly because he thought unlike the rest of his relations, and partly because, being short of stature and destitute of personal graces, the carnal pleasures in which his neighbours and acquaintances took so great delight were for him wholly destitute of attraction ; but as years went on and he attained that which to him appeared the highest of earthly prerogatives—namely, the right to tread in

the footsteps of him whom he had in boyhood
selected as at once the type of all that was
noblest in man and the chief religious teacher
of the age—I mean John Wesley—the ardour
of his pious enthusiasm cooled insensibly, little
by little, as is mostly the way with ardour,
pious or otherwise, and albeit in his ministry
he displayed, if possible, increased zeal and
perseverance, and met with proportionate
success—Aunt Rachel being by no means
singular in her opinion that few places were
so blessed in their pastors as Shobdon—there
were times when he almost despaired of his condition, despaired with groans, and even tears.

For this man had been a true servant of
God once—had had it in him to be a martyr,
an apostle, braving all manner of evils for
Christ's sake, just as Tryphena had it in her
to be a religious visionary, the founder of an
order of holy women, of some especial form of
devotion based on miracle, had her days been
other than they were ; had the soil on which
the seed of her weak life had fallen been other
than Wynn Common, shall we say.

The elect at Coatham, Shobdon, and the
country round about called him a second

Paul; and in the matters of eloquence and internal disquietude—the disquietude of one with whom, when good is present, evil is never far away ; of one who, with a mind set on righteousness, is ever hankering after those corrupt gratifications and allurements of the senses, than which no devil is more inimical to the well-being of the soul—the comparison was fair enough ; but there the parallel ceased, grew less justifiable year by year, would continue less justifiable as time went on. A man who, having been clean at twenty, ponders, plans, does at forty as ponders, plans, and does the Reverend Mr. Latchet, is little likely ever to retrace his downward steps. And yet the man wanted to be better, could get joy out of the thought of change, found his greatest happiness in the consideration, the contemplation of a purity so virginal, so profound, so exquisite that it reflected beauty on the soul which reverently beheld it. Surely the material world possesses no monopoly of anomalies.

"Had you a good congregation?" inquired Aunt Rachel, when the tea was dispensed, the eggs cracked, and Mr. Latchet had helped himself to buttered toast.

" Yes," he answered, " very fair. I noticed some new faces."

" Ah !" said Aunt Rachel, " we must soon think about laying the foundation stone of our chapel. A proud day it will be for me when that is built."

" And me," said Tryphena.

Mr. Latchet smiled at her. He had a pleasant smile, benevolent and cordial.

" It will all come in God's good time," said he gently, " meanwhile it is a great comfort to have the barn to assemble in ; only I wish it were larger."

" Yes," replied Aunt Rachel, turning her egg shell upside down, " it seems a strange thing that there should be the church standing empty, or as good as empty ; for what's half a dozen poor deaf old bodies, besides parson and clerk, Sabbath after Sabbath, while we're pinched for elbow-room ?" and her tone was not entirely devoid of irony.

" When does the new vicar come into residence ?" asked Mr. Latchet, taking a slice of cake from the dish Tryphena just then offered him. It was mostly she who looked after the creature comforts of their visitors, Aunt Rachel doing the talking.

"I neither know nor care," responded that lady, elevating her eyebrows and stirring her tea; "they say he's a poor stick in the pulpit. Betty Gear heard him over at Liss back in the summer; but I'm sure it doesn't matter to me."

"There must be something faulty, I think, in the system of education pursued at our universities with regard to candidates for holy orders," observed Mr. Latchet, thoughtfully; "here and there you meet with an efficient shepherd of the sheep, but as a rule they seem so far removed from the interests of their parishioners, and so little inspired with the true Gospel spirit."

"I don't see how you're to make 'em otherwise," was the resigned rejoinder, "seeing the bringing up they get in nine cases out of ten: let to swear and drink and hear all sorts of shocking loose talk from their very cradles, as it were."

"Yes; and yet the Popish system, which trains its priests in the service of the altar from their youth upwards, can scarcely be considered fortunate in its results. It is a very difficult question, unless you take your stand as we do on personal religion."

"Certainly," agreed Aunt Rachel, "as difficult as making bread without dough. There can't be two doubts about that. They seem to be in a bad way in Ireland, in spite of all this parade and fuss about the King's visit; for my part, I can't see what he wanted there, more can Jacob."

"I suppose he wishes to be fair and treat every one alike," adventured Tryphena; "that is until they have done something to deserve disgrace."

"Deserve disgrace, indeed!" echoed Aunt Rachel, contemptuously. "A parcel of idolatrous Papists. I've no patience with such whitewashing of iniquity. If they want to be treated like Englishmen, let them renounce their errors, and do as Englishmen do."

"Still," interposed Mr. Latchet, mildly, "we must concede a little to religious conviction. Remember, the work of conversion is not always performed in exactly the same way. One soul accepts salvation the very instant it is offered; another seeks the Cross painfully, with many a hindrance, heavily burdened. As it is with individuals, so with nations—Ireland may yet repent her of her sins, and obtain forgiveness ; but hardness and illiberality are scarcely calculated to initiate penitence."

This he said, being a man of wide learning and great understanding, and moreover possessed of a sufficiently accurate knowledge of the workings of the human mind, knowledge only to be acquired by the patient, unremitting study of that exceedingly complex organism in disease and health, and therefore rare.

"Then you go with Mr. Canning!" exclaimed Aunt Rachel, with the air of one who sits face to face with some crushing calamity.

"Only as far as civil liberty is concerned."

"Ah, well," said she after a pause, "men understand these things better than women, but I still stick to my opinion."

Mr. Latchet smiled. Had he given utterance to the thought evoked by that remark he would have observed, "Was there ever a woman who didn't?" But experience had taught him that occasions do now and then arise when a momentary silence is worth hours

of wise and witty dialogue, and he sat
mute.

"What do you think John Tapp said?" inquired Tryphena, with a demure smile, finding
that conversation waned.

"What?" demanded Acts, straightening
himself up in his chair, and otherwise betoken-
ing renewed animation.

"That he hoped the murdered man—— No,
the man who has been so nearly murdered,
was a Papist, because you might then 'try
your 'and at convartin' of un,'" with subtle
mimicry.

Mr. Latchet laughed aloud, and he was not
prone to laughter.

"No!" smiled he, "did he really? What
queer people those Tapps are!"

"Tryphena should not repeat what was
said quite among ourselves," interposed Aunt
Rachel, coldly; "John intended no disrespect;
of that I feel very sure."

"Of course not, of course not!" exclaimed
the minister; "but still they are queer.
Excellent, and in every way admirable; but
still queer."

"They have served us for over one hundred

years," replied Aunt Rachel, as if that fact alone should preserve them from any taint of eccentricity, "counting from John's grandfather; and truer, more faithful friends no man could have. Such persons are above being made fun of."

"I had no idea that I was saying anything funny," retorted Tryphena, moist of eye and red of cheek, "or I should not have said it. The idea of my making fun of John!"

Mr. Latchet gazed at her sympathetically.

"The tongue is a sad traitor," said he, with a sigh—"unruly as old ocean, and fatal as a sword. Do you think this poor young man would like to see me?"

"Eh?" ejaculated Aunt Rachel, startled by the suddenness of the query.

"Do you think this poor young man would like to see me?" reiterated the minister, blandly.

Tryphena furtively blinked away two tears. She loved Martha, and she revered John next to her father; to think that she should be accused of trying to seem sharp at their expense—it was very hard.

"No," replied Miss Fowke, after a medita-

tive pause—" I don't. Not that I would willingly hinder the good work, but the doctor
said he was to be kept very quiet, and one
knows from experience that the sight of a
stranger is upsetting when one's sick."

" Yes — yes — quite so," responded Mr.
Latchet, rising from his chair, " I merely
asked because I never like to waste an opportunity. You must please make my best com-
pliments to your brother."

" But you aren't bound to run away directly?" said Aunt Rachel, civilly, her severe
face softening to solicitude.

" Yes," he answered, glancing at Tryphena,
who was looking out of the window at a black-
bird which had just alighted on the lawn,
" I'm afraid I must. It is already five minutes past six "—consulting a substantial silver
watch—" and I should not like to keep my
good friends at Coatham waiting."

" It is a long walk for you," observed Aunt
Rachel, almost sadly ; " and all this rain we
have had lately has made the roads so heavy."

" We must take the bad with the good,"
rejoined he, cheerfully, " persuaded that in
smooth ways and rough we are equally the

objects of our Heavenly Father's love. Let us pray."

Without a word, it being usual for the minister's visits to terminate on this wise, they all three knelt down and repeated the Lord's prayer. Then followed a short extempore supplication, in which a safe recovery from his illness was besought for the man upstairs, also a new heart and contrite spirit; and then the apostolic benediction having been pronounced, they, after a brief pause, rose up, sober-faced and calmly happy, to shake hands and say good-bye, as much like Christians as was well possible, I think, allowing for their ignorance of cathedral music and the ruinous condition of canon law.

"I fear there are no flowers worth having in the garden," remarked Tryphena, as Mr. Latchet put on his hat; "I was in hopes that I might have got you a bunch, but what with the wind and the rain, they've all gone to pieces."

"Oh, thank you," replied he, quietly, "those you gave me on Thursday are still quite fresh. They stand on a little table by my arm-chair, a treasured link between the past and present. I could not bear to part with them yet."

A faint pink pervaded the girl's soft cheeks, a shy, tremulous smile curved her pretty lips. She looked wonderfully fair, a sweet, tender, opalescent creature, whom it would be little less than sacrilege to associate with things lower than herself, to condemn to come in contact with the filth and harshness of this world, a creature whom it might well be counted for righteousness in a man to love.

"Well," observed Aunt Rachel, trying to seem unconcerned, and only succeeding in looking cross, "it does seem a shame to throw the poor things away before they're done for, I allow, after having robbed 'em of existence."

"Quite so," said Mr. Latchet, opening the door; "that is just my opinion. Good-bye, again. It doesn't rain now."

"Good-bye," said Aunt Rachel, and once more shook hands with him. But Tryphena stood still where she was.

"Come," exclaimed Aunt Rachel, with her usual sharpness, when the hall door was closed, "are you going to moon there all night? Those tea-things won't walk off into the kitchen of their own accord, neither will they wash themselves up, as I suppose you know."

"I was thinking," replied Tryphena, mildly, " that it's time for the gentleman to take his chicken broth again."

But Aunt Rachel said " Pish !" and forthwith betook herself upstairs.

Is it possible that she harboured a doubt of her niece's veracity ?

CHAPTER V.

MONDAY dawned bright and clear and cold.

Tryphena, with the hopefulness natural to very young people, always felt glad at the commencement of a fresh week ; not that it was ever likely to inaugurate any perceptible change in her way of living, to bring her either good news or bad. From exterior interests she seemed as completely cut off as though she were in reality that little lonely may-bush on whose thorny branches she had hung so many fancies, from whose vicissitudes she had drawn so many parables. But the future is a rare corrector of crudities. The self of to-morrow seldom betrays those incon-

sistencies, those faults of temper and judgment so unpleasantly noticeable in the self of
to-day. To-day we have retrogressed, to-
morrow we progress. To-morrow is the gate of
heaven; that gate whereof the posts are humility and perseverance, and the key repentance.
There is no saying too much of to-morrow.

Fact, too, on this particular Monday seemed
inclined to join forces with expectation. Dr.
Sprague declared himself quite astounded at
the advance made by his patient during the
night—an advance due, Aunt Rachel averred,
to some six hours of sweet sound slumber,
and the consumption of a glassful of that
jelly heretofore mentioned—jelly made in strict
accordance with the directions contained in a
receipt bequeathed to the Fowke family by
Thirza, third wife of Tobias, Tryphena's great
great-grandfather, who was a young man in
the time of the Monmouth rising, and narrowly escaped being hung, drawn, and quar-
tered by reason of a fugitive rebel being discovered by a detachment of " Lambs " sound
asleep under one of his hayricks.

The doctor nodded and compressed his lips
as he courteously heard out this assertion.

Jelly was an excellent thing in its way, and so was sleep ; but rhubarb and calomel—rhubarb and calomel, my dear madam, with a pinch of magnesia—two every night for a week, and three if occasion demanded—that was the medicine—that was the elixir ; egad, yes—the doctor rather believed you.

And downstairs things were no less flourishing. Twenty eggs did Tryphena find in the hen-house that morning, counting those three used at tea last night—twenty eggs, fair and spotless, and the fowls seemed likely to lay again, a circumstance which justly occasioned her no little exultation, for the poultry-yard, being under her special jurisdiction, such money as she could make by the disposal of its produce fell to her share, enabling her to do many little unostentatious acts of kindness among her poor neighbours, and contribute towards the support of her heroes, the missionaries, which was to her a source of joy—she being but poorly educated, and contented to see little else than the duty straight before her—if so be that she could see that clearly.

Aunt Rachel, too, though brisk of step and

prompt, not to say abrupt, of speech, according to her wont—old Mrs. Fowke, her mother, used to assert that "you might as well expect snow with a south wind as a soft word from Rachel"—was inclined to graciousness, and a certain lenity of opinion concerning one's mode of mixing dough, and shredding cabbage for pickling, to say nothing of plucking and trussing a partridge which John Tapp brought in on his way to the stable, "thinkin' as it were summat like a sick chap's dinner," not wholly ungratifying.

Besides, "father" would be back by supper-time.

To one already conversant with Jacob Fowke's manner and appearance, it might seem something short of credible that his presence could confer satisfaction on any one innocent of design on his pocket—specially would it seem monstrous that a young and tender woman could derive joy from the thought of his return, or could be troubled by his absence. And yet so it was. The Grange, never too lively, seemed to Tryphena less pleasurable than usual, bereft of its master; the hours when he was away at Coatham,

Chadlington, on one of these business excursions, extending sometimes over two or three days—excursions, the gist of which not even Aunt Rachel knew of a surety, Jacob being averse to unnecessary candour—dragged with quite leaden lassitude. To hear him announce his approaching departure filled her soul with heaviness ; to know that another night would not bring prayer and rest without his good-night kiss made her break forth in voluntary songs, left the words of her favourite hymns upon her lips, thrilled her core through with purest pleasure.

Truly a strangely constituted and not easily to be accounted for young woman !

Whether Farmer Fowke was as fond of his daughter as his daughter was of him remained an open question with those best qualified to judge. When she was a little child he would take her on his knees, and brushing back the golden curls from her broad fair forehead, admit that she " had a look of Amy," that she did in some respect " favour her mother ;" but as she grew up his affection, such as it was, became more and more undemonstrative, and now but for that nightly

salutation — the memory whereof was so
fraught with joy—a stranger staying at the
Grange might have easily remained unaware
of their relationship, or at the most imagined
them guardian and ward, rich relative and
pauper dependent, so frigid was the man's
form of speech, so timid the girl's manner.

And yet Tryphena loved her father—loved
and honoured and believed in him as the best
of masters, the wisest of parents, the most
irreproachable of Christians. That he was a
little stiff with her—stiffer for instance than
John was with Martha—was nothing; must
be ascribed to his habitual gravity, his inclination to interior mortification. That he occasionally seemed disinclined to answer when
spoken to, or when forced to reply by the
exigencies of circumstance did so in a tone
which an illiberal critic might have called
surly, was as a mote in a sunbeam when compared with the sum-total of his virtues. What
did it matter if in the village men called him
griping and hard to please ? Men in the village drank too much cider and gave each other
contused eyes and broken noses. What could
their verdict be worth ?—the breath whereby

it found utterance.   Under his own roof Jacob
Fowke's excellences shone with redoubled
lustre by reason of the hostile and derogatory
remarks passed upon him in the Shobdon Arms
and the " That Alters the Case " beerhouse
on Saturday nights and such other festivals as
necessitate the emptying of mugs and pockets.
If ever man being alive profited by the evilness and scurrility of his generation, that man
was the potentate of Shobdon Grange.   Such
is the force of silence and a preoccupied expression of countenance.

Thus the reflection that he would be back
by supper-time materially and with good cause
heightened the brightness of this cloudless
and singularly happy Monday, bringing a sense
of security and comfort not easily equalled
as a provocative of pleasurable emotion.

To Tryphena that is.

Aunt Rachel, by reason of superior wisdom
—the result of natural endowment and some
five-and-forty years of varied experience, to
say nothing of a mental habit of separating
the essential from the accidental, which
seldom fails to dwarf impressions and check
the flow of sentiment—perceived that there

were items in the programme of reinstallation
which, ineffectively dealt with, might render
that touching and oft-repeated ceremony a
source of something less than unmitigated
delight.

Jacob Fowke was not fond of making fresh
acquaintances; strangers he ever eyed with
distrust and dislike. It was with difficulty,
and after much persuasion, that he could be
induced to extend hospitality towards the
minister on his assumption of those ambassa-
dorial duties for the discharge of which he was
so eminently fitted, although now no firmer
adherent to Mr. Latchet's teaching, no warmer
admirer of his striking gifts, could be found
throughout the county. Gentlemen, who by
birth and education possessed the right to
rank as his superiors, without reference being
made to their principles or condition in the
sight of God, were, above all, the objects of
his detestation. To sin was bad, but to come
of an old family—a family with a Norman
name, and broad acres wrested from the godly;
a family well represented in the pages of
" Burke" and " Debrett," the younger members of which considered propriety well dealt

by if they spent their days 'twixt fray and feast, whilst the elder occupied high places to the furtherance of iniquity and the oppression of the elect—was worse. For the sinner there was hope ; for the aristocrat there was none. How, then, would he face the tidings that a stranger—and not only a stranger, but one whose accent, person, manner, attire, indisputably proclaimed him to be well born—had been floated on the tide of fate, as it were, clean across his threshold, clean upstairs, into the second-best bedchamber, there to remain weeks at the very least—Dr. Sprague said it might be months—there fixed immovably, so that any attempt at ejection would unpleasantly resemble crime.

"If only his name wasn't Valoynes," said Aunt Rachel, turning away from the supper-table, on which she had just placed a dish of stewed pears, to look out of the window, now stained crimson by the fast-lessening rays of the setting sun, and passing on to the mental consideration of the economic and pecuniary side of the question (speech seldom faithfully reflects thought)—"if only his hands weren't so white, and he didn't wear a frilled shirt !"

"Eh!" exclaimed Tryphena, who was, as usual, deep in the renovation of the family wardrobe, "of whom are you speaking?"

"I'm so afraid your father will blame me," pursued Aunt Rachel, plaintively, beginning to feel the effect of protracted mental debate and sorting of arguments; "and yet what could I do?"

"Do you mean about this gentleman?" inquired the girl, searching for a shirt-button in her work-box.

"Yes. What else could I mean?"

"But why should father blame you?" pursued Tryphena, mildly, "I am sure he would be the last person in the world to refuse succour to a suffering fellow-creature. Besides, you say the young man seems amiable, and anxious to give as little trouble as possible."

"That may be," allowed Miss Fowke; "still I wish——Hark! isn't that the gate?"

"Yes," exclaimed Tryphena, reddening with quick pleasure, and hastily throwing her work on the table—"I thought he'd be here before dark;" and she hurried to the door.

But scarcely had she reached it when it

opened, and Jacob Fowke entered, tall, dark,
compressed of lip, sedate of mien as when he
took his departure on Saturday afternoon.
Few people ever saw any change in him, and
those few were to be found neither among his
relatives nor retainers. A gloomy-browed,
keen-eyed, grim-visaged person this cultivator
of cereals and breeder of sheep and oxen—a
person whose outward life is easier dealt with
than his inner.

"Tapp took the horse; I met him at the
gate," said he, in a low, hoarse voice, unbut-
toning his thick black riding-coat, and pulling
a pistol out of each pocket. He seldom rode
unarmed, having once, some twenty years ago,
been stopped by three foodpads as he came
home from market on Christmas Eve, and
eased of his purse and watch. Dull, hard
natures, though slow to receive impressions,
seldom fail of retention when once impressed.

"And how are you?" inquired Tryphena,
possessing herself of his hat and scarf, and
raising herself on tiptoe to kiss his cheek,
"It seems such a long time since you went
away. I suppose because so much has
happened?"

Mr. Fowke knit his heavy black eyebrows.
What was the girl talking about ?

"That is always the way with you, Tryphena !" exclaimed Aunt Rachel, in a tone of
irritation, helping him out of his coat, greet-
ings of the special and demonstrative sort
being considered mere waste of breath at the
Grange—"blaring out everything at a moment's notice. One would think you hadn't
got the sense you were born with !"

"Well, but it will have to be told some
time !" responded the delinquent, who was apt
to betray a certain boldness and breadth of
opinion in the parental presence, scarcely con-
sonant with that spirit of meekness she held
so desirable.

"Yes, but there's a proper season for everything," was the dignified answer ; "besides,
you're not the person to speak."

"But," said Mr. Fowke, pulling down his
waistcoats—he wore two, a black one and a
brown—and frowning harder than before,
"what is there to speak about ? Has a mur-
rain broken out among the beasts, or have the
ricks been burned down ?"

"No, no," replied Aunt Rachel, deprecatorily; "nothing of that sort. Everything's just as you left it, thank God, except the cat, which kittened last night. I told Tapp to have 'em all drowned but one—there were nine; but you must be hungry," and she turned to the supper-table, "I dare say you have had a long ride!"

Jacob's mouth tightened; he was of opinion that the less people meddled with what did not concern them, particularly the doings and intentions of their neighbours, the more likely they were to pay due regard to what did.

"My ride has been as long as I chose to make it," answered he, dryly; "I shall not eat until I have heard what has occurred during my absence."

Thus adjured, Aunt Rachel briefly narrated the events of Saturday evening; "and," said she, humbly, in conclusion—the most intrepid of us own a master somewhere, either inside or out—"I hope I've not done wrong, for, so far as I had any choice given me, it being all so sudden, I tried to please the Lord!"

Mr. Fowke, who had hitherto preserved an appearance of unruffled and even stony composure, here turned away and walked to the window.

Aunt Rachel looked at Tryphena, and Tryphena looked at Aunt Rachel, then Aunt Rachel shook her head meaningly.

"You see, father," began the girl, who for all her gentleness was no coward, neither given to petty reprisals, "aunt was so taken to—Tapp didn't give her a moment, as you may say, to consider—and "——

"Why couldn't you send him to the Vicarage?" interposed Jacob sharply, turning short round, his face full of displeasure, his light blue eyes bent on his sister; "or, if they wouldn't take him in, to Coatham? There's the hospital there. I don't see why my house is to be turned into a "——

"But he would have died from loss of blood, father," exclaimed Tryphena, colouring with shame for his insensibility and lack of charitable warmth; "you would surely not have wished that?"

"Hold your tongue," answered he, harshly, "I was not speaking to you. Do you wish to sup on bread and water?"

"It is just as I said it would be," said

Aunt Rachel despairingly; "and a nicer young gentleman I'm sure no one could see, nor a more grateful; but what does that matter?"

"Mighty little, truly," observed Mr. Fowke, with an ugly sneer, "when one has to find him in board and lodging gratis for weeks. Where was he wounded?"

"In the left shoulder," replied Aunt Rachel, wiping her eyes with her apron. "Dr. Sprague extracted the bullet at exactly five minutes past one on Sunday morning, and a horrid-looking thing it was. It's now in a cup on the mantle-shelf. You can see it, if you like."

"Pooh!" ejaculated Jacob, with coarse promptitude; "what should I want to see it for?" and then he turned again towards the window, and, clasping his hands behind him, seemed lost in thought.

The women meanwhile maintained a grave and decorous rigidity of limb and feature, equally favourable to the modification of human ire and the mute supplication of Divine support. But Mr. Fowke cared little for the expectations of his fellow-creatures, except when

he felt certain of being able to disappoint
them. Having reflected as much as he pleased,
he betook himself to the supper-table, said a
short grace, bade Tryphena draw a jug of
cider, and commenced a meal which, to judge
from its commencement, would neither be
scant nor lengthy.

"Who's that?" inquired he, making a second
assault on the beef-steak pie before him, as
some one came downstairs.

"Martha Tapp," answered Aunt Rachel;
"she's been sitting with Mr. Valoynes. I was
obliged to get some one to help me—not being
able to be in two places at once."

"Humph!" ejaculated he, as Martha entered
the kitchen, "it's a pretty state of things, to
be sure. A man might as well have a second
family."

"Good-evenin', sir," smiled Martha, dropping a curtsey; "glad to see you 'ome again."

"It's about time I was home, I think," was
the gruff answer; "we must get the sign up
to-morrow."

"What's that?" said Martha, looking
puzzled.

Mr. Fowke laughed, and carved a hunch of

6—2

bread. It was not his way to wear ideas threadbare.

"I suppose you want me," observed Aunt Rachel, brushing the crumbs off her lap, a proceeding which brought Beauty out of her corner to court capricious Fortune; "is he awake?"

"Yes 'm; and askin' for summat to drink."

"There's a bottle of French brandy in the cupboard," said Mr. Fowke, "and ten dozen of port in the cellar. We don't keep claret—being new beginners."

"New beginners!" echoed Martha, opening her eyes with wide amazement. "Whatever is the maister talkin' about?"

"You may well ask that," remarked Aunt Rachel, rising from her chair, her eyes on the table, her face pale and grim.

But the master only laughed, and gave Beauty a bit of crust, which, after much mumbling, she rejected as beyond her powers of mastication, being tender-mouthed and almost toothless. When Jacob Fowke was in one of his humours—was bent on being funny —remonstrance and persuasion fell alike pointless on his ears.

With a sigh, Aunt Rachel took a jug from
the dresser, and followed by Martha, who
from a mental table of indications, registered
at intervals during some score of years, perceived that serious disturbances might be
apprehended in the domestic atmosphere of
the Grange, went away upstairs.

For a while Tryphena and her father sat on
in silence, he sipping cider, and occasionally
smiling, as if amused by his own thoughts;
she making a pretence of eating bread and
jam, being in that high-strung and excitable
condition when to do anything, even choke,
seems preferable to utter idleness.

Presently, however, the growing darkness
necessitated movement, and, gently laying
down her knife—Jacob was singularly averse
to noise—she got up to procure a light.

" What did your aunt call this man ?" inquired he, abruptly, turning himself about on
his chair, and stretching out one leg.

" Valoynes," she replied—" Robert Valoynes."

" Has he said anything about himself—who
he is—where he comes from ?"

" She told me this afternoon that he was a

north countryman, and that he had been
making a tour through England to find out
exactly for himself what was the condition of
the poor ; but nothing more."

" Humph !" grunted Jacob—" more fool he.
Did you see the minister yesterday ?"

" Yes ; he took tea with us. We did not
go to meeting, because Aunt Rachel thought
it would make the people inattentive—that
they would be staring at us instead of minding their prayers."

Jacob indulged in a low chuckle.

" Your aunt's got a good opinion of herself,
I will say," observed he, dryly, taking a pinch
of snuff. "It's well for the Almighty that she's
alive to look after His interests."

" I'm sure she does her best," returned
Tryphena gravely ; " and it is not easy to
please every one."

" No," said Mr. Fowke ; " you're right
there. It isn't ;" and then, rising slowly, he
took his hat and went out on his nightly
rounds.

CHAPTER VI.

LIKE TO A SMALL BEATEN BIRD.

NOT until the second Wednesday after Mr. Valoynes' arrival at the Grange did Dr. Sprague show any signs of shortening the term of his imprisonment, or modifying the severity of those recuperative measures which he had considered necessary to guard against a relapse—no inconsiderable amount of local inflammation having exhibited itself at the opening of the case.

" I won't hear of it, my dear sir," had been his unfailing answer, when Robert, who, like most young men, hated enforced idleness only a degree less than enforced labour, suggested that he should get up and try to walk about a little. Lying in bed day after day was weakening in itself; besides he began to feel the want of fresh air and change. " I won't hear

of it for a second. Stay you where you are.
Change, indeed! I'm quite sick of the very
word. People rushing off here and there to
all the four quarters of the globe—Rome,
Brussels, Vienna, Botany Bay—God knows
where—spending their substance on paltry
Belgians, and Germans, and Italians, when they
might stay comfortably at home, and make the
fortunes of their countrymen. Pshaw!"

And Aunt Rachel, who, you may be sure,
was never very far off during the progress of
these colloquies, she esteeming it her special
privilege to carry out the doctor's instructions
to the letter, the more obnoxious they were
to the patient the easier she found them of
performance, being keenly alive to the benefit
obtainable from a judicious use of sickness
and the least palatable kinds of physic—Aunt
Rachel would assume an aspect of grave indignation, and remark " Yes, indeed!" with
emphasis. It was quite wonderful how much
she and the doctor seemed to have in common,
considering the varied nature of the funda-
mental convictions whereon they based their
hypotheses.

But on this Wednesday to which I have

alluded, whether from the reappearance of the sun, who had, as Mr. Fowke phrased it, lately turned from an old friend into an "illustrious stranger," or the eccentric conduct of the wind, which had suddenly forgotten to blow, or the dropping in of two rich patients, neither of whom could reckon with any show of justice on a speedy convalescence, during the preceding day—for some cause, or combination of causes, the doctor's manner evinced a certain alteration, a suavity, if one may so put it, calculated to awaken hope, and widen a man's expectations.

"I think it seems much milder this morning," observed Robert, with fine indifference, sinking back among his pillows and pulling up the bedclothes.

"Yes," replied the doctor, smiling meaningly—"yes, it is very much milder. The wind—what there is of it, that is—is south."

"Really!" remarked our dissembler, and fell to regarding the ceiling.

"I don't suppose you'd care to venture downstairs quite so soon," pursued the doctor, glancing slyly at Aunt Rachel, who just then came in, with a basin of beef-tea in one hand and a letter in the other; "but if you did——"

"No!" exclaimed Robert, starting up, his pale, sharpened face aglow with sudden delight—"I am to have back my liberty——"

"Not unless you will promise to use it wisely," said Aunt Rachel, laying the letter on the bed, "and be content to do little at first, and more by degrees. That came just now. Our postman's getting old and shaky, but I shouldn't like to see the bags taken away from him; though, as my brother says, he'd be better off in the almshouse. But habit's a deal with old folks."

"It is with all of us," observed the doctor, walking to the window; "the cerebral movements are essentially automatic. If Mr. Valoynes"—turning towards her—"does go downstairs this afternoon, I should advise his sitting in the kitchen rather than in the parlour, and above all make him keep out of draughts. I would not answer for the consequences if he were to take cold."

"You hear that, sir?" said Aunt Rachel gravely, stirring the beef-tea.

"Eh!" said Robert, looking up from his

letter, the which he was perusing with avidity
—it was from Matthew Thwaites, the steward,
his father's valued counsellor, his own most
trusty friend—" Eh !"

" You are to be sure and keep out of
draughts."

Robert laughed.

" I will do anything !" answered he, cheerfully, " if only I may be allowed the use of my
limbs and a taste of solid food. Why, how
long is it since I made your acquaintance,
doctor—something like a fortnight ?"

" It will be a fortnight on Saturday," said
Aunt Rachel, giving him the basin, " or rather
on Sunday, for it was not till midnight that
we heard the gray trot up the lane. How
thankful I was, to be sure !"

" Your friends must be greatly relieved to
find that you are out of danger," observed Dr.
Sprague, slowly returning to the bedside, his
highly-coloured countenance expressive of a
delicate and far-reaching sympathy.

" Yes," replied Mr. Valoynes—" yes, I suppose they are. It is seldom well for the servants when a property changes hands conti-
nually. Too many cooks spoil the broth."

"I hope yours is to your liking, sir," interposed Aunt Rachel from the fireplace.

"Quite," he answered, taking a spoonful, "it always is."

"Your place is in Westmoreland, I hear," said Dr. Sprague—"near Windermere?"

"Yes," replied Robert—"that is, it is within a walk of the lake."

"You are a fortunate young man," smiled the doctor, putting out his hand with the air of one who ungrudgingly conferred a favour he could ill afford, "I envy you. Good-morning."

"Good-morning," replied Robert, submitting his fingers to that generous clasp, and therewith the man of medicine took his leave.

"I wish I'd seen your father before he went out again," observed Aunt Rachel some fifteen minutes later, looking into the scullery, where Tryphena—her sleeves rolled high up above her pretty dimpled elbows, her gown skirt pulled through her pocket, her wavy dark hair all tucked away except one stray little curl, in a hideous kind of nightcap—was engaged in the arduous occupation of cleaning knives.

"Why?" demanded she, pausing to bestow minute scrutiny on the blade of that now in hand.

"Because then I could have made sure of his being in to dinner punctually. I want to get the kitchen clear in good time this afternoon. Mr. Valoynes is coming down for a bit!"

Tryphena's cheeks flushed red as the Virginian creeper garlanding the window. In her meek way she disliked strangers as much as did Jacob, particularly male strangers, and Mr. Valoynes had already taken shape and voice in the eyes and ears of her imagination.

"But he will sit in the parlour," rejoined she after a pause—"won't he?"

"No," answered Aunt Rachel; "the doctor says not, for fear of draughts. I wonder where your father is?"

"In the potato field," replied Tryphena, going to work again on her board; "I heard him tell Tapp he'd be down there before long to see about the spreading of some manure. If you like, when I've finished these, I'll put on my bonnet and run down—'twouldn't take me many minutes."

"Ay do, that's a good girl," said Aunt

Rachel; "bring him back with you if you can, for it's nigh on twelve now, and there's not much heat in the sun after three." This on her way into the garden.

Tryphena made haste. It was seldom that she got the chance of a run before dinner, and the forenoon was her favourite time of day. Everything—by everything this unsophisticated young woman meant the cows, and dogs, and horses, and butterflies, and hollyhocks, and asters, and sky, and sun, and children, and dickybirds—looked so bright and wideawake in the morning, before the dust could settle on the leaves, before fatigue could tarnish smiles, and dam the glad stream, than which no water of Pharphar or Damascus, no Jordan is more healing, of rippling childish laughter. To saunter down the lane, now rich in blackberries and whiskered clusters of still tender hazel-nuts, to climb the stile and cross the little sparkling stream, pausing, perhaps, to pluck a bunch of watercresses as one goes, to be warm and free, and in motion, seemed to her rarely pleasant. She made haste.

But expeditious as she was, and quick as

she walked—to run she did not dare, knowing
that a flushed face meant senna tea, or if the
current of ill-luck ran strong, tincture of
rhubarb—the church clock had already chimed
half-past twelve, when she reached the field
wherein Mr. Fowke was superintending the
labour of John Tapp and his assistants.

" Hulloa!" exclaimed he, as she made her
way towards him over the rich, umber-tinted
earth, strewed with the roots and plants of
recently dug-up potatoes—" what have you
come after ?"

" Aunt wants you to come in to dinner at
once," was the prompt answer ; " Mr. Valoynes will be down presently, and she would
like to have the kitchen clear for him to sit
in."

" Let him sit in the parlour," said Jacob,
gruffly.

" No," returned Tryphena, " he mustn't do
that—Dr. Sprague says so ; it's too cold."

Mr. Fowke removed his broad-brimmed
straw hat, took thence a large red pocket-
handkerchief, wiped his face therewith, returned each to their original position, and
stared hard at nothing.

Tryphena abode his pleasure with dumb humility, as might Beauty, who sat panting at her feet, an object of respectful attention to a small, short-haired, rust-coloured terrier, belonging to John Tapp, whose name was Chummy, and sagacity phenomenal.

"Well," said he, after a while, looking round at her suddenly, "why don't you go home?"

"I thought perhaps you'd come with me," replied she, meekly; "Aunt was putting the chops in the frying-pan when I started."

"What does that matter?" demanded he, wrathfully; "damn the chops! Just you go back and tell your aunt that when I want my dinner I shall come for it, and not a moment sooner. A pretty thing, truly, that I'm to be driven and flown at, as if I was a child or a simpleton, because some rascally fine gentleman chooses to turn my house into an hospital. I've heard quite enough of Mr. Valoynes lately—more than I care to hear again. The sooner he gets out of my place the better."

"Father!" exclaimed Tryphena, not a little shocked by this unwonted outburst of bitter-

ness, for let the tenor of Mr. Fowke's reflections on the acts and characteristics of his
neighbours be what it might, condemnatory
or otherwise, he seldom indulged in the dangerous luxury of untrammelled and forcible
expression.

"Ay," rejoined he, with sarcastic deliberation, "and I mean what I say too. Don't
you think that you can make a fool of me, because if you do you're mistaken—the pair of
ye !"

"But I'm sure no one ever dreamt of such
a thing," whimpered Tryphena, moved to
tears, partly by fright, partly by indignation,
at being subjected to so unjust an imputation ; "I'm sure aunt will be quite sorry
that she sent me when I tell her that it has
vexed you. Don't, Beauty !" pushing away
the old dog, who, being rested by this time,
ventured to draw attention to that agreeable
and important fact by standing on her hind
legs, and endeavouring to lick her best friend's
face.

"Let her !" said Jacob, grimly—"let her !"
and then he turned himself about and walked
slowly away to meet Tom Tapp, who had just

been despatched by his father to inquire what
was to be done with the "dressin' as weer
left over;" not because that excellent man felt
himself unequal to cope with this tremendous
question, but because from the master's tone
of voice he felt pretty sure that "Miss Phenie
weer a gettin' it," and therein discerned cause
for pity.

Scarce able to see for sorrow, Tryphena
hastened home. No eyes had she now for the
"fairies' cloaks" hung out to dry on the long
grass beneath the hedges; the comical young
frogs hopping about the road, whereon Beauty
would pounce as greedily as though she had
changed sex and nationality and were a
Frenchman; the divers familiar sights common
to every lane in England whereon she always
loved to look, and which yielded her so many
sweet and lovely thoughts; no ears for the
singing of the birds, the tinkle, tinkle of the
tiny brook. A cloud had veiled her sun—
"Father" was wroth with her.

"Well!" exclaimed Aunt Rachel, when at
last she regained the house—"well, and a fine
time you've been gone, to be sure!"

"I couldn't be any quicker," answered the

girl wearily, untying her sun-bonnet, and sinking down upon a chair. "I wish I hadn't
gone at all."

"I dare say you do!" was the tart response
—"just like your laziness!"

"No," replied Tryphena, with a great sigh
—"no! my laziness has nothing to do with it.
Father was so angry."

"Oh, indeed!" said Aunt Rachel, giving
the chops a final sprinkle of pepper and salt
and sage before she took them off the fire;
"and what might he be angry about,
pray?"

"I don't exactly know. I think it was
because I told him that Mr. Valoynes was
coming down this afternoon, and yet he
seemed most put out at your sending me to
fetch him into dinner; but——" and Tryphena
paused, feelingly, "he said 'damn!'"

"More shame for him," enounced Aunt
Rachel; "he ought to be downright ashamed
of himself. The idea of his calling himself a
Christian, and giving way to nasty, evil tempers like that; but I'm not a bit surprised,
for damn was the first word he ever said.
I've heard mother tell how upset she was

time out of mind. Folks used to say that
the child would never come to good, and worry
her so that she had no peace of her life, till
she took heart one day, and laid the matter
before God in prayer."

" I think grandmother was very foolish to
care what any one said, when she'd got her
own senses to guide her," replied Tryphena;
" but it always hurts me to hear bad words.
Besides, one should be very tender of another's
conscience. Father would not have got angry
of his own accord. It is quite dreadful to
think how much one has to answer for."

" Dear ! dear !" exclaimed Aunt Rachel,
impatiently, emptying a saucepan full of potatoes into a vegetable dish on the table ;
" what a mountain out of a molehill !
You'd better come and eat your dinner while
it's hot, instead of sitting preaching and
groaning there, with a face as white as a mag-
got."

Thus strenuously invited, Tryphena arose
and set a chair for herself at the table. As
she did so, heavily-booted feet came up the
garden path.

" There he is !" exclaimed Aunt Rachel,

who had just clasped her hands in preparation for the saying of grace; "we had better let him ask a blessing. Mebbe 'twill ease his mind."

The door opened, and in came Jacob, gloomy-browed, close-lipped as usual. Tryphena's heart beat fast; she longed to know how he looked, but she did not dare to raise her eyes. Aunt Rachel maintained a devotional serenity of aspect, creditable alike to her self-control and power of abstraction.

In silence she motioned him to his seat—in silence he obeyed the gesture.

"May the Lord in His mercy accept our humble and hearty thanks for these His gifts, and be pleased to add thereto a knowledge of the truth, through Jesus Christ our Lord," said he, and down they sat—a family party of three to outward seeming, a triad of strangers in reality—strangers as strange, as separate each from each, as though one were a native of Borneo, another of Caprera, a third of Patagonia.

The edge of his appetite blunted by the consumption of much pork, potatoes, and cold suet pudding—consumption effected rapidly,

without reference to the wants of others (as I
have said before, hollow ceremony found no
favour at the Grange)—Mr. Fowke, having
ascertained by personal inspection that the
cider jug was empty, pushed back his chair,
got up, and observed, his eyes bent on the
floor :

"I am going to Coatham."

"Indeed!" said Aunt Rachel. "What to
do ?"

"The more you knock under to him," said
she one day when old Mrs. Fowke exclaimed
against the way in which she answered Jacob
back when he spoke to her, "the more you
may. And the man isn't born who shall
make me his bounden slave."

So now she preserved an expressionless
stolidity of visage and cheerful asperity of
tone, soothing or the reverse, according to
temperament.

"What I please," replied he, turning to
the door.

"That you always do," rejoined she, calmly,
"trust you for that. I asked because I
wanted to send a message to the minister
about Hannah Beer, who, I hear, has taken a

turn for the worse, and isn't expected to recover."

"It isn't likely that I shall see him," answered Jacob ; " but if I do I'll tell him to give the woman a call. Have you got any hot water to spare ?"

"Yes," said Tryphena, jumping up, and possessing herself of a jug—she was so anxious to make her peace, to regain the parental favour—"plenty."

"Stay, though," exclaimed Aunt Rachel, whisking round towards the fireplace, " I shall want all that's in that kettle for Mr. Valoynes. I filled it on purpose."

Jacob smiled.

" It seems to me," said he, slowly, "that Mr. Valoynes is master of this house."

" It seems to me," responded Aunt Rachel, " that you're in a very un-Christian frame of mind this morning—flying at the poor girl, and abusing me behind my back. I don't like such crazy ways, and you may know it."

" And I don't like a man who's no more to me than that cat"—pointing to an attenuated tabby kitten which had just taken a seat on the window-sill—" coming and sticking him-

self under my roof, and ordering everything
and everybody right and left, so that I'm
fair turned out of my own kitchen, and can't
have a jug of hot water when I want it."

"Lord bless the man!" cried Aunt Rachel,
hurried into profanity by growing indignation
—"him and his hot water! One would think
every drop cost a guinea. There!"—snatching
the jug from Tryphena, and filling it to the
brim—"perhaps you'll be contented now!"

"No," was the solemn answer, "it'll take
more to content me than that. I don't say
much, but I have my thoughts all the same."

"It would be better if you said more,
I think," rejoined Aunt Rachel dryly; "a
body might perhaps make out what you
meant then, whereas now it's nothing but
hinting and guessing and growling from
morning till night."

"Oh, aunt!" interposed Tryphena, deprecatorily, noting that her father's face had suddenly turned curiously white, and that his
lips trembled.

"But it is," pursued Miss Fowke doggedly;
"and I'm fair sick of it—and that's the truth.
Grudging a poor sick soul the bed he lies on,

and the bit of food he eats ; when he's willing
to pay for it, too. I call it downright dis-
graceful."

" How do I know that he will pay it?"
remarked Jacob, coolly, his face still yellower
than its wont, but his mouth firm. " How do
I know that some day, when he's feasted and
drunk himself strong again, he won't mount
that fine nag of his, and ride off anywhere—
nowhere—leaving me the poorer by Sprague's
bill, and victuals no end ? First he'd been
stripped of every copper he possessed ; now
he's rolling in riches ! What dependence is
to be put on the tales he chooses to tell ? He
may be a highwayman himself, for all we
know !"—with a downward curve of the lips,
significant of humour.

" He a highwayman !" echoed Aunt Rachel,
contemptuously ; "as well say you're one
yourself. Besides, it isn't true that he was
stripped of every copper he possessed, and
that you know—only you are so shocking
contradictious. I've told you already how he
served the fellow who attacked him, by giving
him a made-up purse stuffed with tissue
paper instead of bank-notes—nasty villain.

I only wish he'd got a bullet or two into the bargain."

"A rogue's a poor chap—when he's found out," said Jacob, sententiously, again turning towards the door; "afore that there's few to equal him."

"In his own opinion, maybe!" responded Aunt Rachel, who in common with certain other eminent persons possessed a strong liking for that conversational delicacy, the last word; "but I'm wasting breath. Come, stir up, child," addressing Tryphena, who was putting on her washing-up apron.

To do well and diligently that which she found it necessary or agreeable to do at all, was with this girl as much a habit as to say her prayers when she got up of a morning, or read a chapter of the Bible before she undressed at night. By the time that Jacob reappeared, re-shaven, in his second best coat and nankeen breeches, with a voluminous yellow handkerchief wound about his throat, and huge black boots garnished with spurs— reappeared in his usual town attire, ready to start Coathamwards, not a plate was out of order, not a crumb to be seen; a bright

little fire blazed and crackled merrily on the
hearth, the kettle hummed beside it, the
sunshine streaming in through the diamond-
paned window, flung flickering shadows on
the sanded floor, and lit small tongues of
flame in every metal dish-cover. An old blue
china jar, full of dahlias and fuchsia sprays
and red geraniums, stood on the white deal
table, together with a work-basket and box.
Beauty lay asleep underneath.

A grave satisfaction stole over Mr. Fowke's
countenance as he took it all in. He had
seldom seen the old kitchen look pleasanter—
more in accordance with his innate convictions
of what should be. The old kitchen, wherein
one was rocked in one's cradle, whipped in
petticoats, lectured in trousers ; where father
used to tell how Admiral Anson, with one ship,
beat the Spaniards and captured a galleon
worth a million and a half; and how King
George bullied his wife and children ; where
mother sat and spun till three days before her
death, being a hale old lady, and tough, like
all Fowkes—the old kitchen.

" Tryphena !" called Aunt Rachel from the
head of the stairs a few minutes later, when

he had mounted his stout brown horse and was riding up the road, "where are you?"

"Downstairs," was the prompt reply, given shrilly.

"Have you got the back door shut?"

"Yes."

"And is everything straight?"

"Yes."

A brief silence—then a sound as of a person, of two persons in the act of descent. Tryphena paused, needle in hand, to straighten her black stuff apron, and to determine the set of her flowered chintz frock. She was neat, she hoped, and clean she knew, but it was a terrible thing to sit in the same room as Mr. Valoynes, nevertheless.

"Now, sir," said Aunt Rachel, seeming to support some one, "suppose you rest a bit. This is quite a journey for you."

And some one seemed to accept her counsel.

Tryphena clasped her hands.

"In quietness and confidence shall be thy strength," whispered she, and blushed pink as a dog-rose.

Aunt Rachel's purple lustre made music in the passage.

"This way, sir, if you please," said she; "there is no step, but you must take care not to hit your head. The doorway is rather low."

"Ah !" said some one, "that is always the way in old houses ;" and Aunt Rachel entered the kitchen.

"Set a chair, Tryphena," said she, standing aside to let some one pass—"and shake up the cushion on the sofa. Mr. Valoynes will be glad to lie down presently. You have seen my niece before, sir, though I dare say you don't remember."

"Yes, I do," replied Robert, halting on the threshold, and regarding "my niece" with eyes wherein bland amiability mingled with surprise—"she wanted me to drink some brandy."

And "my niece" dropped him a curtsey.

CHAPTER VII.

STRAYED.

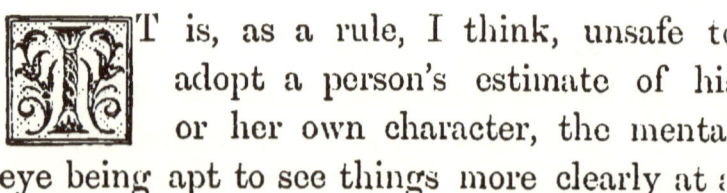IT is, as a rule, I think, unsafe to adopt a person's estimate of his or her own character, the mental eye being apt to see things more clearly at a distance than when close, especially when that mental eye is young, and unskilled in the discernment of proportions. Thus had Aunt Rachel suffered herself to become the mirror of those aspirations and intentions whence Mr. Valoynes, during the tedious hours of his illness, drew sustaining convictions of his own magnanimity, profundity, and dissimilarity to the majority of his fellow-creatures, in itself no despicable proof of greatness, she might have been the innocent cause of leading at least two persons into error, and ensuring

them disappointment more or less poignant,
according to the scope of their receptive
faculties. As it was, however, she, by stu-
diously limiting herself to those facts reverted
to by Tryphena—namely, his northern origin
and curiosity concerning the condition of the
operative and agricultural labourer, subju-
gated fancy, and kept the way clear for dispassionate criticism, when dispassionate criticism should be needed, as steadily as though
she were a tried veteran in the ranks of reason,
and skilled in the management of public
opinion as an Opposition leader.

Nevertheless that those facts adequately
represented Mr. Valoynes' claims on the consideration and reflective powers of the persons with whom he came in contact, I am in
nowise inclined to maintain. The youngest son
of a poor Westmorland squire—the Valoyneses
lost the major portion of their property at the
time that Lords Lovat, Kilmarnock, and Bal-
merino lost their heads, and for the same
reason, being staunch followers of Prince
Charles and High Churchmen, to the babe
crowing in his cradle — Robert Valoynes
absorbed Jacobite opinions with his mother's

milk, and a distaste for existing institutions, notably the House of Brunswick, from the hour in which he first lisped " God save King Henry." Strong of limb, as he was comely of feature, a ruddy-cheeked nut-brown lad, with eyes keen as a hawk's, blue as an iris, in spite of his dark skin, and long light curls — the Valoyneses were ever a swart-browed, fair-headed race ; fiery, too, as the chargers which bore them, sire and son, wherever the fight raged fiercest, wherever the blood-red crest might serve as rallying-point for those to whom one Scottish eagle was worth ten million German rats—strong of limb as he was comely of feature, I repeat, this pauper scion of an ancient and gallant family speedily, however, found in the breaking of ponies, the slaughtering of otters, the shooting of grouse and black cock, and drawing of badgers an outlet for such superfluous energy and destructive zeal as he might have at his command.

Already even in his native county, within the shadow of Scawfell, on the shores of tree-girt Windermere, that curse of modern days, *nil admirari*-ism, had exercised its soul-

degrading influence. To feel acutely on the
score of anything less widely useful than food,
exercise, and money had already assumed the
complexion of mental aberration. The squire,
enfeebled by age and intemperance—men in
the north still drink copiously compared to
men in the south, but at that time not to go
to bed drunk, and well drunk, every night of
your life was dangerous alike to reputation
and social standing—the squire, then, enfeebled and "daffling," as Maggie, the old
housekeeper, who had been madam's maid,
expressed it, had but two desires in the
world ; one of which was that Tom, the heir,
and apple of his eye, might "teach those
scoundrelly Frenchmen what it was to cross
swords with a man whose father had changed
cloaks with the Prince," and having adminis-
tered that salutary lesson, return covered with
glory and whole-skinned to reap the reward
of his endeavours in the admiration of his
country, a gold medal, and the undisturbed
possession of such of the ancestral acres as had
escaped the vengeful clutches of the Crown ;
and the other that Bob—fine, handsome, dare-

devil Bob—should take to his books, and go
to Oriel when ripe for that experience, and
grow up an honest man and a gentleman, by
which the squire meant a red-hot Tory and
one given to sport, as all his forbears had been
before him.

But neither of these ambitions, moderate as
they were, were destined to acquire complete
fulfilment. Tom Valoynes fell at Quatre Bras
side by side with Ensign Christie, the heroic
standard-bearer of the 44th, a bayonet in
his loins and two bullets in his lungs. The
Duke hid his face in his hands when Dr. Hume
on the following morning mentioned his name
amongst those who had perished in that
memorable fray; for the Valoyneses made rare
soldiers, every man of them. And Robert,
instead of journeying south, on academic study
bent, soon found himself, by the death of his
father—grief having effected that which years
and recklessness could not—the master of his
own fortunes, and rather in need of that commonplace knowledge which enables a man to
discourse with authority on the rotation of
crops and the best means of reclaiming waste
land, than skill in dialectic or an accurate

appreciation of the relative merits of Thucy-
dides and Lord Clarendon.

Still, though fully alive to the importance
of personal supervision in all matters pertain-
ing to the comfort of others, or one's own
material advancement, having from his
boyhood been a believer in thoroughness, and
prone to self-help, Robert, it must be con-
fessed, fell short of the ideal country gentleman in one important particular—he was fond
of reading ; would as lief sit indoors of a
winter's afternoon, with a volume of Rous-
seau or Voltaire, or Scott, or Smollett, or
Burns to bear him company, as go for a trudge
over the moor, or skating on the mere, or
shooting larks, which was indeed very unnatural and even monstrous of him, and caused
remark not only in the servants' hall and
stable-yard, but in the boudoir of my Lady
de Moleyns herself, and the dining-room of
the very Reverend the Archdeacon. Nor did
the enormity end there. If it had, public
opinion, though outraged, might still have
been appeased by judicious hospitalities and
the happy selection of a wife. As it was,
there seemed little hope of the present master

of Kirton ever attaining the popularity which
had for generations cast its golden ægis over
that fortunate individual; for not only did
this misguided product of a degenerate age
read when he should have been decimating
the fowls of the air or describing eights for the
entertainment of his lady friends, but he
actually understood, enjoyed, and digested
what he read, deriving thence no small enlightenment on certain points generally in-
vested with a graceful obscurity—such as the
unequal distribution of property, the causes
of crime, the arguments in favour of a repub-
lican form of government, and the like, and
in divers and sundry manners laying up vast
stores of wrath to come.

So matters went on for some five years,
Robert attending to the cultivation of his mind
—by which somewhat vague term he, I think,
understood his progressive and aggressive
instincts—and his property with a fine im-
partiality, productive of the goodliest results,
and the county growing more and more con-
vinced of the necessity for unanimity of action
and the magnanimous forgetfulness of private
differences, if he was ever to be reclaimed and

made to wince wholesomely under a sense of his own evilness.

" When a young man allows himself to be carried away by the shallow trivialities of a parcel of foreigners," said Dr. Bytham, the rector of Waddington, with a stipend of twelve hundred a year, and canon of Preston, besides being the patron of some half dozen small livings, which comfortably provided for the increase and maintenance of the minor members of the Bytham family—" when a young man allows himself to be carried away by the shallow trivialities of a parcel of foreigners," said this eminent and highly-to-be-respected gentleman, turning his back to his study fire, a coat-tail under each arm, and gazing loftily at Mrs. Bytham, who was making out a list of guests for her next dinner-party, " the best means of curing him of his folly, and, one may say, wickedness, is to leave him to himself. Bottle him up ; give his fine atheistic notions no chance of escape—bottle him up."

" Y-e-e-s !" replied Mrs. Bytham, a little dubiously, mentally weighing a half-pay Indian colonel and a justice of the peace—

"but then there's Kirton : one can't afford to lose one of the nicest places in the neighbourhood."

"When duty calls," responded the doctor, "reason should be dumb."

"That's all very well," was the mild reply, rejecting the colonel; "but with three girls still unprovided for, a thousand a year is not to be sneezed at, especially when the man is a gentleman and moral."

"There is no hurry," answered Dr. Bytham. "Remember, Louisa will not be twenty till next spring. If you will only take my advice and show Valoynes by your manner that his opinions are not to be tolerated in decent society, he will drop them ; but, of course, I am nobody."

"I don't know," observed Mrs. Bytham ; "you certainly brought Beauchamp to his senses. I believe Felicia would be still on my hands at this very moment if it had not been for you. I must think it over."

But despite the rigidity with which the doctor's counsel was ultimately adhered to, not only by the female members of his own family circle but by those of all family circles

wherein the name of Bytham carried that
weight and sense of trustworthiness inherent
in the name of one who it was confidently
predicted would be the next archdeacon, and
already possessed the right of nominating six
vicars and dispensing titles to a dozen deacons ;
despite the coldness of old friends, men who
linked Napoleon Buonaparte, the Pope of Rome,
and Charles James Fox together in one stout
bond of iniquity, who regarded Dissenters and
poachers as equally fitting occasions for Divine
wrath, and the honest indignation mingled
with contempt of all virtuous persons, who
swore roundly at their wives and daughters,
and beheld women generally through the
lessening lens of an innate and impersonal
superiority, who, apart from their religious
significance, considered the views advocated
by those writers, in the study of whom Mr.
Valoynes consumed his leisure, wholly wrong
and inexcusable, a gross perversion of the
intellectual faculties, and calculated to turn
society topsy-turvy, so that the carter would
believe himself entitled to a water-tight roof
and meat twice a week, and the carter's wife
to separate beds for her boys and girls and a

dish of tea on Sundays—despite these tokens of right-mindedness, and indications that the spirit of self-sacrifice had not utterly deserted the north-west portion of this island, Robert, as I say, kept on in his own way ; perhaps a little sorry that the line he had chosen diverged so widely from the beaten track, a little inclined now and then to pull up, turn back and seek the high-road whereon one may always be sure of company with what speed he might, still never seeking it, or showing the least leaning thereunto.   Verily, " bottling " did little towards the regeneration of this strange and dangerous young man.

Thus, unable to find among his equals a congenial soul wherewith to consort, he, as might be expected, grew curiously intimate for a landlord and master with those delvers of the soil, those toilers amidst the grain, of whose well-being Fate had nominated him guardian—for that was the light in which he through perusal of Encyclopædical dissertations had come to regard the fact of his accession to the hereditary honours.

" I hear," remarked Lord de Moleyns one

day to his steward—who was generally addressed as " my lord " by strangers, being of
an imposing presence, and fortunate in his
tailor—" I hear that Mr. Valoynes is oftener
to be seen seated by the fireside of some
cottager than at the dinner-tables of his
friends."

" My lord," said Mr. Bantry—the steward's
name was Bantry—" you have been correctly
informed ; nor does Mr. Valoynes' condescen-
sion stop there."

" Ha !" ejaculated his lordship, knitting
his brows as though he would like to know
" where the deuce it did stop."

" Mr. Valoynes is, I regret to say," pursued
Mr. Bantry, " singularly injudicious in more
ways than one. Only last week he refused
to prosecute Tom Fidget, the postman's son—
though the scoundrel was caught by Agar,
one of his gamekeepers, with the hare actually
in his hand—because his wife was ill, and he
had been out of work for the last two months
from abscesses in the arm. I could scarcely
believe my ears when Agar told me."

" Humph !" responded his lordship, who was
a gentleman of few words—" humph !"

"I am sure his father would never have countenanced such absurdity," continued Mr. Bantry, with emphasis; "nor do I call it fair to those gentlemen who have property adjoining his."

"No," was the prompt reply—"no."

"But it is all of a piece—that is, I mean"——Mr. Bantry disapproved of colloquialisms—"Mr. Valoynes seems quite determined to set public opinion at defiance. Whether he is wise, time will show."

"Yes," said Lord de Moleyns—"yes. Quite so."

And then he looked at his watch, and bade Mr. Bantry good-morning. But he felt vexed by what that gentleman had told him, for George, his second son, had been a school-fellow and bosom friend of poor Tom's—he was in the Coldstreams, and got shot at Hougoumont; besides, in an age when cotton and iron, and tallow, and heaven knew what, tried to make itself out as good as blood, it was a thousand pities for the head of one of the oldest families in England to make such an ass of himself.

But—*suum cuique.*

About this time, owing to the continuance of war on the Continent—war which as a tax on our national resources stands happily as yet unparalleled—and the unsettled state of the public mind, which rendered private enterprise little short of hopeless, the hardships and sufferings of the working classes reached a pitch hitherto unknown, undreamt of, even by those who had struggled through the terrible winter of 1797—four shillings a week being the average wages received by the operatives in the manufacturing districts, and bread being sevenpence a loaf.

Deprived by the cruel exigencies of circumstance and the odious selfishness of traders of the bare means of subsistence, the brawny smiths and furnacemen of Manchester soon found a mouthpiece whereby to disseminate knowledge of their discontent in the person of Mr. Hunt. What came of his oratory is now a matter of history. The panic in St. Peter's field — the trampling to death of English women and English children beneath the hoofs of English chargers bestridden by English troopers, are incidents familiar to the memory of every English schoolgirl and school-

boy, and of little weight or meaning, save as
a proof, if further proof were needed, of the
soul-subduing force of colour, and the power-
lessness of numbers.   But when the blood
spilt by the Manchester soldiery still moistened
the soil whereon it had fallen; when the
wounds made by their sabres still gaped red
and painful; when the Peterloo massacre
formed the prime topic of talk in every tavern
and kitchen and dining-room throughout the
length and breadth of the land, it was different.
Men found plentiful food for reflection—no
lack of occasion for brilliance and the utterance of "home truths" in those familiar and
now nerveless facts.   Father quarrelled with
son, and brother with brother over the right
way of looking at them.   One called Hunt
"a low thief," and swore he ought to be hung
"as high as Haman, sir, if not higher."
Another fancied that a little management and
judicious diplomacy might have prevented it
all—there was a way in doing these things.
A third thought the people ought to have
been let to have their say uninterruptedly—
oppressed as they were and ground down.   It
was nonsense to shout under the influence of

patriotism and liquor that "Britons never should be slaves," when the chains were already on their hands and the collars on their necks. Ever so much platform rebellion was better than one secret society. Let Hunt be set at liberty—it was a pity that he ever was arrested. But these sentiments were not common—they were Robert Valoynes'.

Yes ; openly in the market-place, the hunting-field, even the vicar's study, Robert avowed his sympathy with the down-trodden demagogues, waxed eloquent anent the woful inequalities of existence, whereby it was rendered possible that the man who spent his life in making others rich, either mentally or materially, should die of starvation, and be dependent for decent burial on the magnanimity of parochial authorities, whilst the fool, the ruffian, or the egotist wallowed in wealth he had neither helped to get nor knew how to spend ; nay, actually went so far as to question the eternal fitness of what is, and impugn Divine wisdom itself.

For, ardent, clear-sighted, a passionate lover of the Free and True, it needed but some such act of tyranny as this already dwelt on, to let loose the dormant enthusiasm of humanity which had been slowly acquiring strength and volume to the dwarfing and subjugation of every other instinct in his nature, during these years wherein he had dwelt spiritually alone ; and there was never a Valoynes of them all but spoke his mind freely, without reference to place or person, when speech seemed requisite in the interests of candour and uprightness.

That he should adopt this line of action, should thus ruthlessly outrage decency, and, as it were, shake his fist at heaven—for was it not recorded in Holy Writ that the poor should never cease out of the land, that a man should eat his bread in the sweat of his brow, likewise that contentment and a dinner of herbs was preferable to a stalled ox and uncharitable emotions ?—that Robert Valoynes should use this kind of language, and indulge in these kind of speculations, caused little surprise to those who had watched his career since he came of age.

" I have expected it for long," said Dr. Bytham to Lord de Moleyns, taking a sip at his sixth glass of port, and lolling back com-

fortably in his chair—the chairs at the castle
were singularly well fashioned, "when a young
man lets himself be carried away by the
shallow trivialities of a parcel of foreigners,"
with a suggestive shrug. His lordship shook
his head.

"It is a thousand pities," remarked Mrs.
Bytham to milady, as they sat together on the
drawing-room sofa, the young people having
gone to inspect a new fern in the conser-
vatory; "I did hope that when he found
that we all looked shy at him he would have
turned over a new leaf and gone to church,
and—and done as everybody else does," stifling
a yawn.

"Ah!" smiled her ladyship, who was considered delicate, and soon wearied of a subject,
"yes, one might really have thought so too;
but things turn out so oddly. Do you know
I quite envy you that sapphire? It always
puts me in mind of one the Princess Wittien-
stein used to wear as an agraffe at the side of
the head, so"——

Nor did Robert in any way endeavour to
weaken his claims on the adverse criticism of
his friends. Before long he had allotted a

small but tolerably fertile farm to three of the
steadiest labourers on the estate, the said farm
to be cultivated and managed on the co-operative principle for the joint benefit and support
of all three families. If this plan answered
well, he had some notion of trying it again
elsewhere on a larger scale, being bent on the
amelioration of at least one of those social
difficulties—namely, the degraded and painful
condition of the agricultural labourer, into
which he entered so keenly, and the consideration of which had already wrought such un-
foreseen and startling effects upon his way of
life and outlook.

By the end of May, eighteen hundred and
twenty-one, a week after his twenty-sixth
birthday, he had started on the tour which
ultimately ended, for a time at least, in Goose
Lane, in the parish of Shobdon-cum-Shacker-
ley, in the county of Dorset—a tour under-
taken, as Tryphena told her father, to find
out exactly for himself what was the condition
of the poor throughout England; a tour the
motive of which was assuredly a lively
philanthropy, but the result—if not an
untimely initiation into those mysteries

whence Dr. Bytham so confidently asserted
would stream full and complete elucidation of his knottiest puzzles — who could
tell ?

CHAPTER VIII.

AS CLAY TO THE SEAL.

IT was surprising how quickly the inmates of the Grange lost all sense of strangeness—became familiar with their uninvited visitor; how speedily the uninvited visitor habituated himself to modes of speech and living foreign to his previous experience as those prevalent among the natives of Central Africa, or the seal-skin clad denizens of Labrador. Even Mr. Fowke, though for the first three or four afternoons that Robert left his room and joined the family party in the kitchen, inclined to silence, and rash in his dealings with hot tea and the crust of bread, also the prey apparently of a pernicious modesty which forbade his looking straight at any one, or sitting still a moment longer than was imperatively necessary, even Mr. Fowke, I say—gradually permitted his shyness to be lulled into quiescence by this docile young man's urbanity, and ultimately admitted that "for a gentleman there was nothing much amiss with him."

For Mr. Valoynes was indeed very docile and very urbane—so much so that he was sometimes quite startled, not to say annoyed, at his own weakness as he chose to call it.

"If I stay here much longer," said he to Aunt Rachel, one foggy morning, when she had successfully dissuaded him from venturing out into the garden until the sun should have pierced the golden haze now obscuring his iridescent majesty, "I shall some day find myself back in long-clothes, and sucking at a pap-bottle. You are the most determined woman, Miss Fowke, that I ever met with."

"When it's a question of common-sense and right," retorted she, stoutly, stunning a luckless blue-bottle with her duster, "I own I am hard to get over. No square has more than four sides."

That this mathematically-minded and obdurate person should find cause for approval in her nursling was not wonderful—nay, the wonder would have been had she not; he being her nursling, and she being herself.

"Dr. Sprague may take all the credit to himself," observed she to Tryphena, "but I know better. I know that under the mercy of God he owes his life to my having on the third night used my own discretion about giving him one of those pills instead of two, and tea instead of brandy and water. The improvement to be noticed on the Tuesday morning was something astonishing. Your medical men are always ready to make game of everything a female says or does, just as though we were born fools and didn't know our right hands from our left; but I say, 'let 'em, they'll find out their mistake some day.'"

Thus feeling that Robert did in somewise owe existence to her ministrations, Aunt Rachel took the same kind of interest in his actions and inclinations that a cat might in the leaps and cud-chewing of a leveret which had associated itself with her infant family, and unconsciously intruded within the

sacred limits of her maternal affections. He
was outside her experience, differed as much
from her in opinions, tastes, principles, as a
rodent may reasonably be supposed to differ
from a flesh-devourer; but despite all this
she had busied herself about him, had been
sorry for his sufferings, glad to think that he
was free from pain; the climbing shoots of her
woman's nature had turned towards and laid
hold of him with their little claw-like hands
of kindly thought. He might wrench himself
free—might trot off on that fine nag of his as
Jacob said, and never be heard of more, but
he could never again be a stranger; Aunt
Rachel reigned over him.

Between Tryphena and this object of charitable reflections, the *entente cordiale* was
scarcely so pronounced. For one thing, their
acquaintance was of much shorter duration,
she never having set eyes on him from the
hour that he was carried upstairs to that in
which he came down again; for another, they
were young man and young woman, a circumstance, I find, productive of singularly oppo-
site results, and in nowise to be depended on
as a safe basis for conclusions, which I ascribe

to the fluid and unstable organization of young women.

Nor was this all. A deeper reason underlaid Tryphena's impassibility and even stiffness towards Mr. Valoynes—a stiffness specially apparent when they were alone, as frequently occurred owing to Aunt Rachel's pressing and numerous domestic duties, increased by her temporary slackening of activity, and Mr. Fowke's self-absorption—than scant acquaintance, or lack of years.

He was, if not an unbeliever, still strongly tinged with scepticism—the scepticism which deposed Jehovah of Mount Sinai for the *Etre Supreme* of the Charmettes; which substituted for the arid shores of the sea of Galilee the shallow shingle of the Lake of Geneva; which beheld in the surgeon's scalpel the one divining rod worth credence; in an Act of Parliament enforcing sanitary regulations, and a due attention to the convolutions of waste pipes, the surest revelation of a saving faith; which scorned the joys of heaven and mocked at the woes of hell. Tryphena shuddered as she contemplated the awful doom in store for one who thought such things; the frightful de-

pravity of the heart and mind which could for
a second become the receptacle of the like
imaginations ; shuddered and turned pale, and
prayed mutely that Mr. Valoynes might be
mercifully delivered from his errors—finding
prayer easier than refutation.

Mr. Valoynes, meanwhile, being well-sea-
soned in iniquity, and impervious to rebuff,
exposed his blackness to her whiteness, without stint or scruple. She interested him—so
did Aunt Rachel, and so did her father, for he
was fond of thinking about and analyzing the
motives and mental characteristics of his
fellow-creatures, and these people struck him
as worth study ; but what was curiosity in
their case became pleasure in hers—the pleasure one gets by entering into the beauty
of some chaste and fine design, of contem-
plating the loveliness of some delicate and
unique work of art.

" One could live with a woman like that for
hundreds of years, and never grow weary of
her," thought he one evening, as they walked
slowly, and in silence, homewards through the
fields, from Liss, a tiny village built beneath
a limestone cliff rich in fossils, and situate

about a mile and a half from Shobdon; "how divinely quiet is her face, how exquisitely clear her soul! Tryphena," said he, out loud, slashing off the head of a tall wiggle-waggle —as Dorsetshire children call what we in the north term jockey-grass, from the cap-like form of the tiny seeds—with his stick, and scattering her meek reflections like a company of startled doves, "what are you made of— rose-leaves, like the Hero of Musæus? the scent of lilies and the songs of shells?"

"Pray do not be so silly!" responded she, gravely, "why should I be different from other people? I am made of flesh and blood, like every one else."

But he shook his head.

"I do not believe it," smiled he.

"That does not surprise me," was the calm rejoinder; "you believe nothing!"

That she should occasionally, in her devout zeal for what she held to be the truth, and the only truth, overstep the limits imposed by courtesy on speech, seldom aroused any other feeling in the mind of this hardened infidel than amusement.

Moreover, it was quite right and proper and

in harmony with the simple earnestness of her character that she should see in him one shut out from the tender mercies of the Father, should endeavour in her weak childish way to bring him to a knowledge of his danger.

"What a wife you will make for Mr. Latchet some day, Tryphena!" remarked he one morning, when they had been arguing with greater warmth than usual anent the beauty and justice of wholesale slaughter as practised by Divine command in the days of Saul and Samuel; Tryphena gathering grapes off the vine meanwhile, mounted on a ladder set against the wall, he holding a wicker basket for their reception" (as I have already said, it was quite wonderful how much at home he had contrived to become in these four weeks which had elapsed since his discovery in Goose Lane)—"I dread to picture to myself the condition of the ungodly hereabouts when that hallowed union shall take place!"

The rounded cheek and little ear turned towards him burnt crimson.

"Mr. Latchet has his mind set on other things than marrying or giving in marriage," replied their owner, not without dignity;

" besides I object to light conversation on such a subject."

" That means that you already regard him with feelings of peculiar interest ?" pursued Robert stubbornly, a dry smile upon his lips.

"I do not know why you ask me such a question !" said the girl, turning to drop a bunch she had just snipped off with her big scissors into the basket, not a vestige of coquetry in voice or face—she was as devoid of that spurious sort of modesty which winces at the mention of one man by another in connection with matrimony, as a child ; " I have always looked upon the minister as a dear friend, and one precious to the Lord, and I take great delight in listening to his discourses. Sometimes when he is carried away by what he is saying, his face quite shines like the face of an angel, and there is a kind of a throb in his voice like the noise of waves. Paul, I think, must have preached like that !"

" There is no doubt that he possesses the gift of eloquence," admitted Mr. Valoynes somewhat tardily, scarcely as though he derived satisfaction from the confession ; "but I would rather he did not come here so often all the same."

"He comes to see you," replied Tryphena, with delicious *naïveté;* "he is as anxious as I am, as Aunt Rachel is, that you should share our blessings. He told me so the other afternoon, when I was showing him those Polish chickens father brought home from Chadlington. 'Mr. Valoynes is a man of vast intelligence, Tryphena,' said he, 'and a noble disposition. I like him exceedingly, but his opinions fill me with pity and aversion.' Those were his very words, I do assure you," perceiving an ironical smile creep athwart Robert's face; "I said them over to myself when I woke up at four o'clock the next morning, because I made up my mind I would tell you when I got a chance, and that is my way of remembering things."

"Really!" observed Robert; "of course none of my remarks gain the like consideration?"

"Oh, yes, they do!" answered she promptly; "only this morning I was trying to remember what you said to father last night about the virtue of self-reliance, and how careful one should be never to let the wants of to-day force one into the lie or meanness or perhaps crime of to-morrow, which I thought strange, as you don't believe in God."

" I spell my God with two o's, you see," answered he mildly ; and then he helped her down from the ladder, and she went away basket-laden into the house, to receive Aunt Rachel's instructions with regard to the washing and stripping of its contents, preparatory to their conversion into certain home-made wine, for the successful decoction of which innocent liquor the female members of the Fowke family enjoyed a reputation of unsullied splendour.

From this short excerpt it will be readily perceived that Mr. Latchet had lost no time in making the acquaintance of the distinguished and wealthy stranger—Robert's fortune and position were already accurately well known by other persons than those resident in Shobdon Grange, and in other places than Shobdon —whom Providence had been at the pains to subject to his influence, punishing his body for the sake of his soul. Of the effect produced as yet on this unsuspecting and callous object

of mysterious workings, by the minister's
arguments, supplemented by much lively and
even commonplace conversation, and necessitat-
ing the frequent renewal of brain tissue by
copious applications of strong tea, hot cake,
and new-laid eggs to the digestive organs, it is
difficult to speak with certainty. Mr. Latchet
was clever, and taking him at his own value
as an enthusiast of orthodoxy, well read. Tired
occasionally of matter-of-fact experience, and
the wisdom bred of doing, Robert would welcome the sight of Acts' dark emphatic countenance, as might a romance-loving young
lady that of her favourite author's last novel
after a course of Grote, Sir William Hamilton,
and the "Contemporary Review." To him it
was possible to speak of something a little less
satisfying than the price of wheat, the growth
of foreign fashions, the vices of the aristocracy,
the levities of the queen, without initiating
silence or the gapes. In his youth, too, he
had dwelt in the north, knew the keen pleasure
of a tramp through ling and heather, had seen
the sun rise on a June morning from slate-bound
Skiddaw, and drank of the strong mountain
air, fed on the wild mountain sights. The hill

people were still dear to him ; he liked to hear
of plans for their improvement, mental and
bodily ; he took an interest in the co-operative
farm ; had extended views concerning the
game laws and the Catholic question ; saw
things more as they were, Robert thought,
less distorted and tinged by his own personal
convictions than was common with men of his
stamp — or indeed of any stamp whatever.
They got on together.

Still Mr. Latchet, despite that recorded
speech of his in which the expressions, " vast
intelligence " and a " noble disposition " appeared in such happy contiguity, could not
be quite sure when he was alone and secure
from confusing influences, that Mr. Valoynes
met with his entire approval, even under the
limited aspect of a man of the world and
would-be benefactor of mankind.

" I wonder," observed he to Aunt Rachel,
one Sunday evening as they sat together in
the parlour, Tryphena having gone into the
village to take old Mrs. Goodwin, who was
blind and palsied, a sago pudding, Robert acting as her escort, and Mr. Fowke being " somewhere about" (which meant, as a rule, in the

kitchen with a churchwarden in his mouth)—
" I wonder you are not afraid to let those two
young people be so constantly together."

" What two young people ?" inquired Aunt
Rachel, who had been thinking of something
a vast deal more important in her opinion
than all the young people in Great Britain—
viz., how soon it would be possible to begin
building the new chapel, of which the site
had already been determined—namely, in The
Tumps, a field about a quarter of a mile from
the village on the Coatham Road, and the property of Mr. Fowke.

" Your niece and Mr. Valoynes," replied the
minister, promptly ; " a girl's affections are
easily won."

" Tryphena has been well brought up,"
responded Aunt Rachel, not without frigidity,
arranging her cap strings ; " besides, Mr.
Valoynes, let his opinions be what they may
about working folks and Revelation and such
like, is, I am sure, far too much of a gentleman
at heart to say or do anything behind my back
he wouldn't before my face ; of that I feel
positive."

" Still he is a man, my dear Miss Fowke,"

smiled Acts, deprecatorily, " and Tryphena is
a very lovely young woman !"

" She is very well," was the impassive
answer ; " she has her mother's skin and eyes,
and her father's hair. For my part I like
more colour and animation"—Aunt Rachel had
cheeks the tint of a Quarrenden, and eyes as
bright and restless as a robin's—" and she
might have been a couple of inches taller without its being a dissight ; but you can't have
everything."

" Nor can every lady be Miss Fowke,"
added Mr. Latchet, bestowing a gentle squeeze
on Aunt Rachel's somewhat red left hand,
" luckily ; otherwise we might gradually become neglectful of our treasure."

Aunt Rachel laughed, a little nervous laugh,
and turned away her face ; but the hand he
held trembled.

" Ah, well !" said he presently, with a
reflective sigh, rising from his chair—" we
have much to be thankful for—much. Still
I really would keep my eye on them. It is
always best to be on the safe side ! How long
do you think he will remain ?"

" Do you speak of Mr. Valoynes ?"

"Yes."

"It is impossible to say. I heard him tell Jacob yesterday that he would like to go away for a bit, see all that was to be seen in this neighbourhood, and come back again, but nothing was settled."

"So! Well, I must be off. Say good-bye for me to your brother and our truants."

"Yes," answered Aunt Rachel, following him into the hall. "But we shall see you again soon?"

"Without a doubt; my difficulty is how to keep away. Good-night and God bless you!"

"Good-night!" replied Aunt Rachel, her eyes bent on the floor, her hand lost in his, her heart fluttering as might a maiden's of seventeen.

Another minute, and he had gained the road. But she stood still, there where he had left her; stood still, smitten with shy ecstasy, ready to cry, to laugh, to wring her hands.

When is a woman not a woman?

CHAPTER IX.

RAPIDLY the pleasant autumn days —frost-tipped, but warm at noon —sped by into the past, laden with withered leaves and faded flowers, and not a few regrets. The Virginian creeper burnt flame-wise on the walls, flecking the ground beneath with pale clear red, exceeding beautiful. The Michaelmas goose annually consumed at the Grange had been caught, killed, plucked, stuffed, trussed, roasted, and eaten ; at this latter part of the ceremony the minister assisted with fine readiness and success. The month had changed its name, and Robert Valoynes formally announced his intention of quitting the hospitable quarters wherein he had met with so much kindness, and been

entertained so well, for a while, paying them
another visit on his way back to Kirton,
where he meant to keep Christmas, in order,
as Aunt Rachel had phrased it, that he might
see all that was to be seen in that part of the
country, and thus ultimately accomplish the
purpose for which he came.

"How long do you think you'll be gone,
sir?" inquired she, driving a drowsy fly away
from the cream-jug—breakfast was under dis-
cussion when Robert entered upon his plans.

"Oh, about a fortnight, I suppose," he
answered, with a momentary glance at Tryphena; "from that to three weeks or a
month."

"I asked," said Aunt Rachel, "because I
rather thought of having the bed furniture
and window curtains taken down and washed;
and at this time of the year one can never
reckon on a fine day—for certain, that is—
not but what the weather seems settled
enough just now."

"I almost wonder at your having the
courage to make another start, after your
adventure in the lane," observed Jacob, salt-

ing his porridge; "but that's a stout nag of yours—and you needn't travel after dark."

"No," said Robert, "nor do I mean to. It wasn't in the lane, though, that the fellow fired at me; it was at that turn in the road where you branch off to go to Chadlington, just by the brick-kiln."

"Ah," remarked Aunt Rachel, whose appetite for detail, specially of the sickening and horrific sort, was unbounded—"no wonder you were faint from loss of blood. Why, that's nigh upon a mile from the sign-post!"

"It's rather surprising," said Jacob, looking away out of the window, "that nothing should have been seen or heard of the man since. I mentioned it to the constable, too."

Mr. Valoynes held his peace. The rural constabulary in those days were something less than Vidocqs.

"I suppose I had myself to thank," observed he, presently, with a resigned smile; "if I had not prepared that purse so cleverly, I dare say I should have got off with a whole skin. Indeed, in my own mind I make no doubt that he fired at me more from rage than malice prepense."

"That makes him no less of a villain, though," remarked Aunt Rachel, promptly; "on the contrary, it shows deeper wickedness —for to try to murder a fellow-creature out of sheer spite is surely worse than to have recourse to violence to make him give up his money. I know it sounds strange to argue in this way; but there is no use in blinking things."

Robert laughed.

"I am glad to hear you say that," smiled he. "Fancy your having become an advocate for free thought!"

"Within due bounds," was the cautious answer; "not to the puffing up of self, and putting of the human mind in the place of grace."

"Come," said Mr. Fowke, rapping his horn spoon on the table, "if you two get argufying at half-past seven in the morning, it's not much work that'll be done to-day, and I can't afford to have idle folks pottering round me, unless they choose to pay for it"—with a short laugh.

Truly this good man's notion of humour was a little eccentric.

Aunt Rachel's lips narrowed to a line. Rebuke came hard to her at any time, but to be rebuked before her juniors, before a bit of a girl like Tryphena, and for defending the truth, for uttering that word in season which is as apples of gold in pictures of silver;—she finished her breakfast in silence.

"What day do you think you shall start?" pursued Mr. Fowke, turning to Robert as he rose from the table.

"To-morrow," replied that gentleman. "I may as well take advantage of the fine weather while it lasts. As Miss Fowke observed just now, at this season of the year one must look out for squalls."

"Yes," answered Jacob, thoughtfully—"Yes, that reminds me that the thatch on the biggest rick should be seen to. Humph! Well, I shall be in to dinner about one. You'd better make a pie with them apples Tapp brought up last night, some of 'em looked to me as if they'd got rather bruised; you can use those first."

"Very well, father," said Tryphena, and the working day began.

As usual, when anything had occurred to

ruffle her serenity during those matutinal
hours, so favourable to the growth of pious
resolutions, and the cultivation of a hopeful
spirit, Aunt Rachel's face and temper throughout the morning, and even far on into the
afternoon, until remembrance had been
drowned in tea, were scarcely remarkable
for sweetness, or calculated to allay depression.

It was curious how cross this worthy soul
could look without suffering an additional
wrinkle to appear upon her broad, high forehead—an additional line about her broad, red
mouth. Where the subtle something showed
itself, what that subtle something was, not
even Tryphena, after the amplest opportuni-
ties for elucidation, could discover—but there
it was; and when it was there, the quicker
you could retire into your own inner con-
sciousness—oblivion—the garden—village—
the better for you.

But Tryphena, being doubly essential to the
smooth working of the domestic machinery,
now that Robert's presence necessitated an
advanced style of housekeeping, and the ex-
penditure of much and severe thought on the

capabilities of cold meat and the nature of "relishes," had no chance of flight. She, poor child, must do as she had too often done before—namely, endure patiently unto the end. After all, it was better than it might have been—than it used to be. At eighteen one cannot well be shaken blind, or scourged, or put to bed in the day-time, and fed on bread and water. No, there was some good in growing up, tiresome as it was. One o'clock drew near.

After dinner, at which meal Jacob and his guest had nearly all the talk to themselves, save those questions and answers enforced by individual liking and the position of dishes, Mr. Valoynes asked to have his horse brought round, as he wished to ride into Coatham to call on Dr. Sprague with regard to a certain ten-pound note snugly reposing in his breast-pocket, and also to add divers warm articles of clothing to those which had been already forwarded to him in his portmanteau by the proprietor of the hotel at Lyme, where he had made his last halt before journeying Shobdon-wards.

"Certainly, sir," was Mr. Fowke's ready re-

joinder. He had concluded a profitable
bargain with a butcher who had called to
have a look at the pigs since breakfast, and
was consequently as urbane as his sister was
the reverse—a not uncommon occurrence,
permit me to observe, these good people being
as the ends of a see-saw whereof Tryphena
was the fulcrum; "certainly, sir! Tryphena,
run down to the stable and tell Jim to saddle
Mr. Valoynes' horse at once. He's had his
corn; I saw him fed myself."

" No," said Robert, jumping up as she prepared to obey; "pray don't you trouble. I'll
go."

" But it is no trouble," replied she calmly,
and forthwith proceeded to the door.

" Oh, but you really mustn't !" he reiterated,
hurrying after her, the upshot of which was
that they both went.

Silvertail was a favourite with Tryphena.
Many were the petty thefts she committed on
his behalf, many the surreptitiously-obtained
lumps of sugar, bits of bread, and apples that
he had snuffed up from off the palm of her
small white hand.

" Poor old boy," smiled she, somewhat sadly,

as on hearing the stable door open, he turned his head and gave a gleeful little grunt of welcome.

"Why do you call him poor?" questioned Robert, following in her wake; "to me he always seems the most fortunate of creatures."

"I call him poor," she answered, leaning her head against his neck—a glossy chestnut neck, trellised with delicate veins wherein ran blood noble as his heart—"because he is going away to-morrow."

"In that case," smiled Robert, "I must be poor too!"

"Oh, no!" said the girl quickly; "you are not poor at all; you are—as you always are."

"But why?" he persisted. "We are at least of equal value?"

"I don't know," was the sedate response. "I am very fond of Silvertail."

Robert turned away—a sudden darkness on his face.

"Candid, at all events," said he, rather bitterly.

Then Jim Goodwin, bare-armed, perspiring, redolent of humanity and manure, made his appearance, bridle in one hand, saddle in

another. Confidential conversation became as
the Regalia—the days of childhood—a quiet
conscience. Tryphena bestowed a valedictory
pat on Silvertail's nose, thereby reading that
admirable animal a salutary lesson on the
vanity of desire and blind confidence in the
honourable intentions of others, and went indoors. It would be wrong to give Aunt
Rachel further excuse for the entertainment
of Satan.

But though when he, Robert, on returning
to the house to get his coat and hat, together
with the loaded whip, without which he
seldom rode now, paused on passing through
the kitchen, where she was engaged in cover-
ing sundry jam-pots with brown paper, to inquire if he could do anything for her at
Coatham, she simply shook her head without
looking up, and scarcely seemed to reply to
his "Good-bye," I should fall short of that
high standard of veracity which I have
hitherto so sedulously endeavoured, as becomes
a humble and faithful chronicler, to keep constantly in view, were I to assert that throughout the afternoon the thoughts of this young
woman were without exception thus well

regulated, that Fancy never once showed signs of insubordination.

"Men are better off than women!" said she, with a sigh, looking up into the cloudless sky.

"Why?" demanded Aunt Rachel, stirring the fire—it was tea-time.

"They can do so much more good."

"Or they can talk about it, which seems nowadays to stand for pretty much the same thing."

"No," replied the girl, gravely, "I do not think that. But women are so weak and small in their ideas; besides all their work seems to lie indoors."

"If work's good for anything," answered Aunt Rachel, sturdily, "it's as well done indoors as out. An act is worth just what it is worth, according to my way of looking at it— place don't signify."

"No," responded Tryphena, "that is very true; still it must be nice to be able to go here and there, and always do as one likes—liking to do what was right, of course—without having to ask any one's leave, or think what people would say."

"Ah!" rejoined Aunt Rachel, "I thought that was at the bottom of it. Perhaps you'd like to dress up in man's clothes, and go for a soldier, like old Betty Spurrell?"

"Dear me, no!" smiled Tryphena, "that would not suit me at all. I could not hurt any one to save my life; besides I think fighting wicked. Peter was told to put up his sword. How Christians can go slashing and killing each other after that, I cannot understand; but all men are not soldiers."

"No!" answered Miss Fowke, dryly; "some are thieves, and some are murderers, and some spend their lives in profligacy and intemperance."

"And some preach the Gospel to the heathen, and some give all their goods to the poor, and some spend their lives in redressing wrongs."

"Yes," allowed Aunt Rachel,—"yes; good isn't a matter of he or she. A man may be saved as well as his wife, if God so wills it; though I believe the woman is converted easiest, maybe because she's weakest."

"Talking, as usual," observed Mr. Fowke, who had entered the kitchen at that moment; "talking, talking, always talking! Why isn't tea ready?"

"It is nearly," replied Aunt Rachel, setting forth the tray; "but I thought you'd wait a bit for Mr. Valoynes."

"Mr. Valoynes!" echoed Jacob, sneeringly, tossing his straw hat on to the sofa, "what's Mr. Valoynes to me that I should go hungry for him? Mr. Valoynes!" with fine accentuation.

"Well, he'll be gone to-morrow," snapped Aunt Rachel, seizing on the kettle with the vigour of exasperation.

"And a good thing, too," was the grim answer; "he might have gone sooner without my missing him."

"It's a pity you don't tell him so."

"So I would," thundered Jacob, "as soon as look at him, if I cared to. But I don't—I don't choose to waste breath on him."

"You waste breath enough in being civil to him, though," said Aunt Rachel, stoutly, taking the sugar-basin from the cupboard,

" and you're glad enough to have his money. I don't like such double-facedness."

"You hold your tongue," commanded he; "I'm master in this house, and I do as I choose. Get the cold meat."

CHAPTER X.

HEN the occasion of this brief explosion of rancour, which, like some foul gas, being generated in the dark places of the mind, there circulates in noxious obscurity till converted into deadliest flame by the ignitive force of an incautious word; when Robert, to discard metaphor, regained the Grange, the old eight-day clock was striking six, and the day-labourers in field and byre and barn were trudging home along the silent lanes, their worn, tired faces red with the fading brightness of the setting sun, their minds for the most part set on food and sleep. True, Peter Batt, who lost his wife last week—she was sixty years of age and he is sixty-five, and they married young;

but bread must be eaten, be you glad or sorrowful, in this most weary world, and the man who would not end his days in the work-house must cut short his weeping—old Peter, I say, may occasionally lift his sore eyes to that ruddy heaven, and wonder vaguely where be Joan, and how she, who could never go three steps up a ladder without turning giddy, do contrive to keep her head "up theer;" and Ben Sogden, whose daughter Polly—he has but one—lies sick of a fever, hard at death's door, with "nowt but the neighbours to look to for nursin'," Mrs. Sogden having lost the use of her limbs from rheumatics, may quicken his pace every now and then, and make a face like a man who is in need of consolation ; but these are exceptions. Indeed, when one comes to think of it, the eighth, or tenth, or twelfth part of nine shillings is not much to be gay and picturesque and proverbial upon.

And yet these dull souls had most of them a "good-night, zur," for the stranger, whom it was rumoured, "weer a great man in 'is own parts, and good to the poor." How all-sufficing is the language of a kindly eye.

"Where is Tryphena?" inquired this great

man, when, to oblige Aunt Rachel, who still
regarded his well-being as in somewise dependent on her exertions, he had swallowed
a cup of tea and two ginger biscuits, and was
at liberty to look about him; "I hope she
has not got one of her headaches." This he
said knowing her to be subject to such exhibitions of nervous weakness, a weakness which
refused to yield either to Dr. Sprague's opium
and calomel, or those infusional remedies
wherein the sweet of established excellence
mingles so effectively with the sour of a her-
baceous growth.

"No," replied Aunt Rachel, "there is
nothing the matter with her this evening, to
my knowledge—she is in the orchard, I think,
seeking for the fallen apples. I told her she
might have them for Dicky Ludlow, if she
pleased, and she set off directly. Dicky's a
prime favourite of hers. He's that deformed
boy, you know, sir, whom you may have seen
sitting on the churchyard stile. They tell
me he'll sit there from morning to night,
grinning, and crooning, and saying all manner
of nonsense. A merciful thing, I say, if the
cart that went over him had crushed his head

instead of his legs, or if he'd died in the
small-pox last summer, both for his mother,
who is a widow, and himself, for life can be
nothing but misery to one who's got neither
sense nor health ; but she can't be brought to
take that view, poor woman. 'I never had
but one boy,' says she, when you speak to her
about it, as I have sometimes, 'and I shall
never have another. So I must make the
best of what I've got ; and he's not so dull
always. On Sundays, when he's got his new
jacket on, and whenever he chances to meet
Miss Phenie, and she takes notice of him, just
smiles and says, "Well, how are you, Dicky ?"
it's quite surprising how sprack he do become.
"Mother !" says he, "the angels have come
again—can't you hear them singing ? can't
you see them ? Oh, they are so white and
beautiful, and they have baskets full of cakes
and apples in their hands !"' Poor lad !"

Robert smiled.

"It is like Tryphena to be gentle with an
idiot, with any creature who is in need of
tenderness and pity," observed he, rising from
his chair. "I think, with your permission,"
courteously—to be abrupt was in those days

a little less than gentlemanlike—" I will try
to find her out, as it is my last night."

" But you are coming again ?" responded
Aunt Rachel promptly, looking round at him
with a certain sharpness. She put full confidence in his sense of honour, but the minister's words still lingered in her memory; he
was a far-seeing man, was Mr. Latchet.

" I hope so," smiled Robert, gradually near-
ing the door—" such at all events is my
present intention."

Aunt Rachel stooped to search for a button,
which had just rolled off her lap. When she
looked up, she was alone.

It was, as I have already said, a lovely
evening, clear, with that peculiar opalescent
clearness seldom seen except directly after
sunrise on a June morning—the most favourable of all times, in my opinion, for the un-
folding and nourishing of the appreciative
faculty—and when the first autumnal frosts
have imparted that invigorating freshness to
the air which strikes so pleasantly on senses
jaded with the too great splendours—if that
may be—of an old-fashioned summer. The
pale new moon, shaped like unto a comma,

floated scarce denser than a cloud over the
yellowed woods—yellowed in the daytime,
and already carpeted with crisp brown leaves,
now dight in atmospheric blue. From the
Grange chimneys floated upwards smoke
plumes—blue likewise, and straight as any
line ; from the cow-yard came a pleasant
smell of kine and new-cut hay. What odour
sweeter than good Dapple's breath ?—Dapple,
who lost her calf before the wheat was cut,
and even now at times will lift her head and
snuff the air and low uneasily, her mother's
heart being tender still. No hen was to be
seen ; Dame Partlet and her lord were sound
asleep, be sure, safe on their perch—heads
hid 'neath wings, side pressed to side, as became so prudent and affectionate a pair.
Peace brooded on the earth. Robert's face
saddened and his eyes grew grave as he perceived the true beauty of that quiet scene, so
tame beside the weird grandeur of his native
moors, so poor compared even to the luxu-
riant fertility noticeable farther west; as a
minuet of Schubert's to a symphony of Beet-
hoven's, a lyric of Longfellow's to one of
Shakespeare's tragedies. Could it be that he

was loath to go, would willingly have lotos-
ate another month away? I cannot say—
idleness is strangely weakening.

But unless he would stand stock-still and
dream at his ease without further reference
to reason or the lapse of time, prolonged meditation presented difficulties, for the orchard
and kitchen-garden joined, and the latter was
of no very vast extent. With a sigh he proceeded on his way. But when he reached the
orchard gate, no maiden could he see. Swing-
ing it back, he stepped into the shade among
the thick-trunked, gray-armed trees—some
giants of their kind, and still endowed with
fruit.

"Tryphena!" he called—it was curious how
quickly he had learnt to address her by her
name, quite naturally too, so that he startled
no one by so doing—"Tryphena!" he called,
putting out his hands—the branches hung low,
and it was almost dark to unaccustomed eyes
—"where are you?"

"Here!" she answered—"don't you see
me?"

"No," he said, glancing to and fro. Then,
suddenly perceiving her on his right hand, he

added, " Oh, there ! I had no idea you were so close !"

" Does aunt want me ?" she inquired, tightening her hold on her apron, gathered up pocket-wise, and weighty, to judge from its protuberant appearance.

" No," he replied, " I don't think so. She was immersed in the mysteries of needlework when I left her."

" Then why did you come ?" This placidly, searching with one foot for additional treasure.

" I thought you would be glad to see me," with mock gravity.

"I do not know why you should have thought that," she answered, just as gravely, stooping to disembed a recent discovery.

He laughed, and remained silent for a while; then he said, as if still smiling :

" Perhaps that was not quite my reason— perhaps I wanted a last quiet talk. We have been so much together, I shall miss you so when I'm away."

"At first you may," she replied, unmovedly; " one's heart gets soft when one is ill. Things and people take quite a different kind of look ; but that soon wears off, and the world turns gray and brown again. I have frequently wondered how you could put up with us."

" My child," exclaimed he, in a tone of deprecation, " how can you speak so ? Why do you think so meanly of your life—this beautiful, pure life, which is an angel's in heaven compared to that led by millions ?"

" I do not think meanly of my life," she returned, " nor of any life except a wicked one. There are nights when it seems dark, but if you will look long enough you will see that the sky is full of stars ; so are the lives of those who, like us, live in silence and obscurity."

" Where did you read that ?" asked Robert, gazing not quite incuriously upon her delicate pale face.

" Nowhere," she said ; " I fancied it." Then growing more animated, she exclaimed, showing him her store, pale gold and crimson and fair russet brown : " See ! haven't I got a fine lot of apples for poor Dicky ?—enough to last him for a whole week. I wish it didn't get dark so quick, I'd run down with them before supper."

But Robert's face betrayed scant sympathy.

"Tryphena," said he, gravely, "I hope you won't be angry; but when I was at Coatham to-day I chanced to see something which rather took my fancy—a sort of locket—and I ventured to bring it back with me, hoping that you would accept it as——"

"Oh, but," interposed she hastily, "you know I never wear ornaments. Aunt wouldn't permit me to for one thing, and I shouldn't like to myself."

"But this is so simple," he argued, producing a small red morocco case from his pocket; "I am sure Miss Fowke could not object to this. See;" and he pressed the spring.

Tryphena, who, for all her self-restraint and upward aspirations, was still only a girl, indulged herself in just one frolic with temptation.

"It's very pretty," said she; and so it was—an oval enamel pendant, the ground deep blue, the design, a beautifully-painted white dove bearing a rose, set round with pearls. "It must have cost a great deal of money."

"What it cost is a very secondary consideration if you like it," rejoined Robert, calmly.

" There is no question about my liking it," she smiled, " that is certain ; and I am very grateful to you for having thought of me, but I cannot accept it all the same," firmly.

" Why not ?"

" I cannot."

" That is nonsense. That is not treating me as a friend. I bought it because I wish you to think of me sometimes when I am gone, not because it was fine or fashionable."

" But I shall think of you without being reminded," replied she, demurely, with a shy babyish smile.

He held his peace.

" What does that mean ?" he demanded presently—" what am I to understand by that ?" and his voice deepened.

" Eh ?" said Tryphena, looking up, her eyes big with innocent surprise.

" You tell me that you will think of me without being reminded——"

" You are very strange to-night," she interposed—coldly—drawing back a little ; " surely in saying that I shall remember you I say nothing very wonderful. I only wish that I could find greater pleasure in the memory— that our acquaintance had been productive of more good."

Robert groaned, thrust the case back into the pocket whence he had taken it, and turned away towards the gate.

"I do not mean to be rude," added she, still in the same chill tone ; "and I trust I have not offended you. I should be very sorry to do that."

"No," he replied resignedly, "I am not offended. Indeed, I suppose I ought to feel rather flattered at your taking any interest in me at all."

"We are told to pray one for another," returned she, "and to try in every way that we can to make plain the truth ; but I am too ignorant, I fear, to be of much use to any one, and yet I have asked God to give me understanding."

"My dear," said Robert, turning himself about, and laying his hand upon her arm—it was not possible for fleshly thoughts to long withstand the volatilizing influence of her purity—"if I am not as good as you would have me—as I might be—I am better for having known you—can never cease to be better."

"Ah," smiled she, shaking her head, "but faith does not mean faith in another human creature, very likely worse than one's self; it means (I am quoting Mr. Latchet) the total surrender of the will and the affections; it is the gift of the Spirit, and the central principle of all real religion."

"Religion," replied Robert, "is scarcely a fixed term. Have you never read those lines of Pope?

"'For modes of faith let jarring bigots fight;
He can't be wrong whose life is in the right.'"

But Tryphena shook her head again.

"If that is true," returned she, "no one need be saved, and the Gospels are just idle tales, like 'Old Mother Hubbard,' or 'Jack the Giant-killer!'"

"Oh, no," responded Robert—"by no means. Merely biographical narratives of more or less value, according to internal evidence and the verdict of contemporaneous history."

"For shame!" she exclaimed, indignantly, "whatever will you say next? Pray let us go home at once!" and she hastened past him to the gate.

He followed her. In silence they regained the garden path. Confronting them rode boat-wise the new moon, now no more vapourish, but bright and sharp of line. Already here and there a star blazed golden on the blue ; the air had freshened, and the bats come forth from cave and ivy-bush and hollow tree to stretch their veined wings. Not many insects were abroad—that is, of the flying and ephemeral sort—but occasionally a great white moth would flutter up from off a cabbage leaf or rhubarb frond. It had been still as Robert came, and now the continuous silence waxed almost oppressive. Some persons bear disappointment best when mute, others get strength from speech—speech frivolous, inane, it may be—having no connection with the cause of their uneasiness.

"A penny for your thoughts, young lady," exclaimed Mr. Valoynes, willing to dilute his own.

Tryphena laughed : she was a sunny-tempered soul enough, when let to be herself.

"I was thinking," replied she, "of the myrtle shoot Martha gave me last August, and wondering whether it would strike, and where I should plant it if it did. You know the best way to raise myrtles is to put a slip in a bottle full of water when the wheat's in bloom ; but they never do well, it is said, unless the person who plants them is proud. So I'm afraid mine will come off but badly."

"Oh," said Robert—"on the contrary, I should consider its future assured."

"But I am not proud."

"Not at all," returned he dryly, and laughed. Was he thinking of his fair friends in Cumberland, I wonder ?

"But I am not," she reiterated stoutly. "Ask Martha, ask the minister, ask even aunt. I do not mind being found fault with justly ; but it is a shame to accuse one of wickedness which is outside one's nature."

To this appeal, however, Mr. Valoynes

vouchsafed no answer. That he was inclined to self-reliance, even in matters usually held secure from the aggressive insolence of private judgment, has, I think, been proved past doubt.

CHAPTER XI.

HE morrow dawned raw and foggy; nevertheless, as the glass still stood at fair, it seemed reasonable to hope that as the day advanced the sun would gradually break through the clouds, and render the first stage of Robert's westward journeyings enjoyable, despite the gloom of its commencement.

Aunt Rachel was astir betimes. To travel on an empty stomach, or an insufficiently stored one, was in her opinion an open breach of faith with Providence.

"If we do our part," said she, rolling a handful of dough in flour preparatory to patting and pinching it into the semblance of a pincushion—the Fowke milk-cakes were a matter of history in Shobdon—" God will do His ; but some folks seems to fancy that He's got a ear for every man's whistle. It's no wonder to me that there's such a deal of misery in the world. Just step out to the hen-house and see what eggs you can find, Tryphena."

Breakfast, with its unusual and sumptuous concomitants, discussed and commented upon —Robert being alternately scolded and coaxed by Aunt Rachel into doing what she called " justice," which being translated signified eating to the verge of suffocation—Silvertail was led by John Tapp to the garden gate, the small knapsack, in which were packed such articles of raiment as were necessary for comfort during a three weeks' pilgrimage, was strapped to the saddle, the silver-mounted and crested pistols, on which the Valoynes motto, " Audaciter," appeared in happy prominence, were placed in the holsters, and, whip in hand, Robert proceeded to satisfy himself that everything was in that taut condition so essential to the success of all expeditions, short or long.

" Woho !" said Jacob, laying a hand on the

horse's bridle, as his master stooped to examine
the girths; "what's your opinion of the
weather, John?"

Screwing up one eye, Mr. Tapp gazed
heavenward with pensive gravity.

"Well, sir," replied he, after a bit, "I
dunno as we shall ev any rain—mebbe a drop
or two 'bout three, just when the day turns
like, but nothin' to speak of."

"That's right!" exclaimed Robert, re-assum-
ing an erect position, and brushing the dust
off his strong, rather large white hands. A
stalwart, broad-shouldered, shapely gentleman was Mr. Valoynes, as he stood there in
the cold light of the early autumn morning,
his keen blue eyes bent on his four-legged
friend, cheerful expectancy the prevailing expression of his clean-shaven, well-featured,
pleasant face—a face which alike tempted confidence and assured sympathy; a face in which
it were hard to say whether intelligence or
kindliness were most apparent.

"That's right!" exclaimed this Don Quixote
of some fifty and odd years ago; "and now
I will go and make my farewells indoors!"

"Very well, sir," smiled Jacob, whose

manner had from the moment of his appearance that morning been remarkable for urbanity, as cheering as it was unlooked for.

But as Robert turned towards the house
Aunt Rachel and Tryphena appeared beneath
the porch—Tryphena looking grave as usual,
also a little melancholy.

" So !" exclaimed Robert, hastening towards
them, " I was just coming to say good-bye !"

" I've put you up a few red lavender lozen-
ges," observed Aunt Rachel, tendering him a
small white packet carefully sealed at either
end ; " they're home-made, so you needn't be
afraid of them ; and for——"

" Oh, thanks !" he interposed, battling hard
with rising laughter, " but I hope I am
beyond the aid of physic now."

" We never can tell what a day may bring
forth," responded she, soberly, permitting him
to take her hand ; " and a stitch in time saves
nine. Besides, there's no need for you to take
them unless obliged. Good-bye, sir, and may
God bless you, and bring you back to us in
safety at no very distant day."

" Thank you !" said Robert, fervently,
squeezing her large-knuckled fingers with

affectionate vigour—she had been very good
to him—"thank you from the bottom of my
heart. I shall always look upon the Grange
in the light of a second home, and my
encounter with the highwayman as the most
fortunate misfortune that could possibly have
befallen me."

And Aunt Rachel smiled waterily and
sniffed, and turned away to wipe her eyes
with the corner of her apron, for she felt
strangely moved.

"Good-bye, Tryphena," pursued he, his voice
scarcely so steady as it had been heretofore.
The hand he held out to her a little less than
even-pulsed.

"Good-bye, sir," replied she, and laid her
pink-tinged palm on his.

"Wish me God speed!" said he hurriedly.

"I wish you God speed, sir!" repeated she,
and smiled up at him.

For a moment, two moments, they stood
thus; then their hands severed, and he strode
down the path.

"I'll take care that your portmanteau gets
to Exeter all right," remarked Jacob, standing aside to let him mount; "I think you

said you should be there in about a week's time."

"Yes," replied Robert dully, settling himself in the saddle and taking the reins; "in about a week's time. Good-morning."

" Good-morning, sir."

"Good-mornin', sir," echoed John Tapp, touching his hat and smiling broadly—"and a pleasant journey to ye !"

"Thank you," answered Robert, dully as before, and rode away.

At the bend of the road—which traversed would shut out the Grange from his view—he turned himself about and looked back; but there was no one visible save John, who was slowly walking towards the foldyard. With a sigh Robert faced round again. Another minute and he was lost to sight.

"There !" exclaimed Mr. Fowke, when the door was shut, and the litter of departure removed, and the kitchen had resumed somewhat of its usual appearance ; " now the place seems to look a bit more like itself again. You needn't cook dinner for me. I shan't be home."

" Where are you going to ?" inquired Aunt

Rachel, whose eyes and nose betrayed acquaintance with the waters of affliction.

"Where I choose."

"Shan't you be in to tea?"

"Perhaps."

"But you don't mean to stay out all night?"

"How do you know? What's that to you? You mind your own business—snivelling fool."

"Ah!" ejaculated Aunt Rachel, as he stumped noisily upstairs, "I may well snivel, I think. There's others that will snivel besides me before long, unless I'm mistaken."

"What do you mean?" inquired Tryphena, looking scared.

But to this query no answer was vouchsafed.

CHAPTER XII.

WITH CHEEKS ABASHED.

"REALLY!" exclaimed Mr. Latchet, about half-past three the following afternoon, as he seated himself on the parlour sofa, and placed his tall beaver hat beside him—he was scrupulous concerning the accuracy of his attire on week-days as well as Sundays, being delicate in his tastes, and aware of the value of externals —"really! and so the phœnix has taken wing at last."

Tryphena, to whom this remark was specially addressed, her aunt having gone to visit Widow Poole, an aged lady, for whom she entertained a deep regard, partly because of her many afflictions, and partly because of her knowledge of simples, which knowledge, Miss Fowke asserted, was slowly being rooted out of the land, in common with feminine modesty and Scriptural doctrine, by the machinations of foreigners and bishops—Tryphena, I repeat, maintained a serene and respectful silence, respectful alike to the absent and the present.

"And I suppose," pursued Mr. Latchet, crossing his short legs and regarding her with an expression of amused curiosity, "you ladies are almost heartbroken in consequence?"

"Dear me, no," smiled the girl, gravely, "why should we be? Mr. Valoynes is a very nice gentleman, for a gentleman—nothing more. Besides, he is coming back again."

"Indeed!" exclaimed the minister. "When?"

"In about three weeks' time, I think. From that to a month."

"Indeed!" reiterated Mr. Latchet.

"He was sorry that you were not at home when he called to bid you good-bye," continued Tryphena, looking up at a blue-bottle which was buzzing in the window—"at least, he told aunt so at supper."

"I was sorry, too," replied Acts, blandly.

"I meant to have given him a piece of advice, which he might have found serviceable."

Tryphena's eyes waxed curious.

"What was that ?" she asked.

"To travel as a bagman. By so doing he would have saved money and secured company. It is surprising, too, how well landlords treat riders compared to other people."

Tryphena remained silent for a while, her face expressing no very acute appreciation of the value of this ingenious proposition. Then she observed quietly :

"I am afraid no one would ever take Mr. Valoynes for a person of that description."

"Why not ?" was the quick retort.

"He is so refined looking, and his ways are so different. But of course I am scarcely able to judge, having seen so little."

"No," replied the minister, gravely—"no ;" and therewith seemed to meditate. "That," continued he, at length, "is the one drawback to a secluded life. It leads a young person to form so many erroneous conclusions."

"And yet," rejoined Tryphena, "I do try to see deep into things."

"I know you do," smiled he, benignly ;

"the worst is, you generally see too deep. There is a point at which the objective and subjective become one, remember."

"Let me see," mused Tryphena, looking puzzled, "what does that mean? The objective is you and the subjective is me, and—but no——" breaking off short, her cheek as red as her lips.

Mr. Latchet laughed, passed his hand across his eyes, and laughed again.

"Philosophical terms seldom admit of extension," observed he, dryly. "Do you think your aunt will be much longer?"

"She is coming now," replied Tryphena, catching sight of a well-known Leghorn bonnet among the shrubs, and hurrying out to let her in.

"Who have you got in the parlour?" inquired Aunt Rachel, as the hall-door opened, kicking off her clogs.

"The minister," answered Tryphena, lowering her eyes, and wishing that her face did not burn so.

"The minister!" echoed Aunt Rachel. "Why, you're as red as a turkey-cock."

"Am I?" was the somewhat hypocritical

rejoinder, " I thought it seemed rather warm. Was Mrs. Poole pleased to see you?" this crossing the hall.

" About the same as usual," responded Aunt Rachel, shortly. " How do you do, sir?"

" How do you do?" smiled Acts, rising to shake hands. " I am glad you have been for a walk this beautiful afternoon ; it will do you good."

" I did not go out for pleasure, though," answered Miss Fowke, selecting a chair with deliberation ; " I should not think that right. Work while there is light, say I, for the night cometh when no man may work, nor woman either. Idleness is all very well for sick folks ; I like to be doing."

" That is evident," replied Mr. Latchet, still smiling ; " no one who enjoys the privilege of your acquaintance may doubt that. Still, an occasional break in the routine of daily duties is essential, I think, to their proper performance. The human mind is not a machine."

" 'Twere difficult to say exactly what it is !" sighed Aunt Rachel, untying her bonnet-strings ; "sometimes it's a sieve, and at others a box no one's got the key of. Look at old Reuben Kempson. When he was young I've heard say there wasn't a brighter, straighter, nicer lad to be found this side of Axminster; and now what is he?—a miserable doiting old critter, with never a word in his mouth from year's end to year's end but curses—squatted up there in the chimney-corner more like a superannuated ape than a human being."

"But then," interposed Tryphena, "that is because he let a friend of his be hung for stealing sheep which he took himself. It is impossible that he should ever be anything but unhappy and morose after doing such a thing as that. Of course the man's face is always before his eyes. Of course he is always living over again the days when they used to be together. I can well understand his not caring to talk or walk, or be like other people."

"I have been told, however," observed Mr. Latchet, "that when he was hale and hearty, he evinced none of this depression. It is since he had rheumatic fever and became a cripple that the full sense of his sin has come upon him—if sense it is, and not just a sulky determination to keep his own counsel."

"Ah," said Aunt Rachel, "he's a curious old customer; 'twouldn't be a trifle that would make him speak if he didn't want to."

"No," smiled Acts; "I never encountered a more obstinate old gentleman. Every time I go into his cottage—and I generally give him a call about once a week—I say, 'Well, Reuben, haven't you got anything to tell me? Isn't there something hidden away in your mind which you'd like to get rid of?' 'No, sir,' says he, staring at the fire, 'nothin' as I'm aweer of.' 'But,' I pursue, 'you've got some secret sorrow. You want consolation and sympathy. I can give you both.' 'Nay, sir,' is the persistent answer, 'I want nowt but bread. Folks do say as I be troubled wi' bad thoughts, but I dunno.'"

"Yes," exclaimed Aunt Rachel, "that's him all over, poor misguided creature. Maybe it would be as well to mention him in prayer. Tryphena, do you remind me this evening. We should never cease to hope—Christ died for all."

"Truly," remarked Mr. Latchet, and grew very grave, so grave that nothing more was said for some little while. Then, with a sigh, Aunt Rachel, rising from her chair, remarked:

"You'll take a cup of tea, of course?"

"No, thank you," said Acts, starting as though roused from sleep, "you are very kind; but I must not stay. Indeed I only meant to look in as I passed, to see how you all were, and whether your visitor had left you."

"Yes," replied Aunt Rachel, reseating herself—she had no wish to speed the parting guest — "he left yesterday, directly after breakfast; and no sooner was he gone, than my brother must needs be off too, so here we are all alone again."

"Dear me!" sympathised the minister, "what a gad-about Mr. Fowke is. By-the-way, do you know I heard a curious little bit of news about him the other day? Nothing to alarm you," perceiving her colour to be on the wane; "indeed, I dare say you know it already."

"No," said she perturbedly; "that is, I have heard no news at all; but then, he does not always tell me what he is going to do."

"Ah, well; perhaps I had better say nothing. After all, it was mere gossip."

"Oh, but," exclaimed Tryphena, "it would be cruel to excite our curiosity to no purpose."

" Be quiet, child !" rebuked Aunt Rachel ;
"you make too free with that tongue of yours.
Some day it will get you into trouble. What
was it, sir, that you heard ?"

"Well," answered Acts, getting up from
the sofa and gazing into his hat, "I chanced
to be at Bridport yesterday. I went to see
an old friend of mine, and after dinner—he is
in the coal line himself—we strolled down to
the harbour to look at the shipping. Having
seen what there was to be seen, and gone over
one or two vessels, we were just thinking
about getting back to supper, when my friend
was accosted by a seafaring-looking man, who
insisted on our having something to drink at
his expense, 'Just for luck's sake,' said he. I
declined, my cloth pleading my excuse, but
my friend had a glass of rum and water, and
then, with much handshaking, they parted.
' Do you know who that is ?' inquired he, when
we were on our way home again. 'No,' I
replied ; 'how should I ?' 'Well,' smiled
Deane, 'he's the captain of that square-rigged
barque lying off there,' pointing to a vessel in
the distance, 'and to-night he sails for Guinea.
He's made one voyage already, and might

have lived independent if only he could have
kept his mouth and spirit-flask apart; but
drink and the persuasions of his partner have
sent him afloat again, and afloat I'll guess he'll
keep till he goes under.' 'And who is his
partner?' I asked hap-hazard, out of pure
curiosity. 'Fowke of Shobdon,' was the answer—'Fowke, of Shobdon Grange.'"

"Lord a mercy!" cried Aunt Rachel; "whatever will the people say next?"

Mr. Latchet laughed—he seemed in a risible
mood that afternoon—but Tryphena scarcely
smiled. It went against her sense of fitness
to know that her father's name—the name
she held superior to all names owned by men
—was thus lightly dealt with by strangers,
persons ignorant of his graces, beyond the
reach of his influence.

"But," pursued Aunt Rachel eagerly, her
face and mind alike quick with anxiety, "it
must be a mistake. Jacob may be close—I
won't say but what he is—but he isn't so
close as that."

"I do not think it is a mistake," responded
the minister calmly; " my friend is not one to
speak without his host."

"But," argued she, "fitting out a vessel—
and if he's a partner he must have gone shares
in the risk—would cost a mint of money, and
I know he's drawn nothing from the bank
more than was wanted to settle the Michaelmas bills, for I was looking at the cheque-book
only yesterday."

Mr. Latchet paused. To throw fuel on the
flame at present would, he fancied, be alike
wasteful and deleterious.

"It is possible," he suggested gently, after a
while, "that your brother may feel himself
called to participate in missionary enterprise.
We all know how sadly Africa stands in need
of the Gospel message, and what great store
he sets on spiritual enlightenment."

"Yes!" exclaimed Tryphena, a lovely smile
playing like sunshine on her face—"yes, that
is it, of course. How dull not to have thought
of that at once! Dear father, I was sure he
must have some good meaning."

But Aunt Rachel remained silent. To Jacob
had she confided the disposition of her entire
fortune—namely, some three thousand and odd
pounds, which had accrued to her at various
periods of her existence, through the deaths of

relatives and the advantageous sales of divers
small portions of the property originally hers
—believing his capacity for business to be such
as became a Fowke ; and this being the case,
to hear suddenly, in no authorized fashion,
round a corner, as it were, that he was spending money like water, risking no one knew
how much precious capital in the interest of
blacks and sea-captains, was not only startling
but horrifying.   That he meant well she did
not doubt—but he should have spoken. There
was something unnatural, unbrotherly, in this
independent way of going on.   She remained
silent.

"Where is Guinea?" inquired Tryphena,
her mind's eye already bent on a scene of bar-
baric beauty, wherein palms, sand, and beaded
savages played no inconspicuous part.

"On the north-western coast of Africa," replied Acts.   "Have you never read 'Robinson
Crusoe?'"

"No," she answered, "but I have heard
of it."

"If your aunt will allow me, I will lend it
to you," he pursued.   "It is a favourite book
of mine, and will give you much information,

not only about Guinea, but other places besides.".

"Oh, thank you," said she. "Aunt, do you hear what Mr. Latchet says?"

"It beats me!" exclaimed Miss Fowke, dejectedly; "I can make neither head nor tail of it!"

"Give it up then," smiled the minister. "Some things are best let alone."

"That may be," was the grave response. "Indeed, I've thought so myself when troubled with much pondering; but practical matters like the selling of stock and victualling of ships can't be put aside like that. They must be looked into and well understood if one's not to go quite to rack and ruin. Just as though there weren't plenty of other good folks in the world beside us. I do really think Jacob must be gone off his head altogether."

"Oh, aunt!" exclaimed Tryphena, and flushed pink as any shell.

"I begin," said Acts, "to feel sorry that I spoke."

"Your speaking or not speaking is of very small consequence compared to the fact," returned Aunt Rachel coolly. "I take small count of words, I do assure you."

"But Mr. Fowke may feel annoyed at my want of reticence," he continued. "Perhaps if you mention it to him"——("If!" interposed Aunt Rachel, with meaning)——"you will do me the favour not to give me as your authority. I should be so grieved to be the occasion of any unpleasantness."

"Unpleasantness!" echoed she. "Things must have come to a pretty pass, I think, if a sister can't ask a brother for an account of her own, without unpleasantness!"

Mr. Latchet smoothed his hat. His mouth was smiling, but his eyes were bent on the floor. Tryphena glanced at him uneasily.

"You must excuse my plain speaking," pursued Aunt Rachel, after a pause. "I have no intention of being rude, least of all to you; but I'm upset, and that's the truth."

"And for that I am extremely sorry," rejoined he, quickly, offering her his hand. "Still, I think you view the matter too seriously, I do indeed."

"It is not necessary, you know, that because a thing is not talked of and made a fuss

about, it should be wicked," said Tryphena,
mildly; "indeed, we are told to do good
secretly, so that our Father, who seeth in
secret, may reward us openly."

"Yes," smiled Mr. Latchet, "exactly.'

But Aunt Rachel's lips moved not, neither
did the severity of her countenance abate.
She had her opinion, and no one could alter
it. It was hard if she had lived four-and-forty
years in favour with God and man, and the
enjoyment of a ripe and elastic judgment, to
be denied the right of criticism when most
needed.

"Those who know most say least," remarked she, presently, rising to her feet.
"When I was a girl it was years that made
wisdom; now it's the want of them. Good-
bye, sir; perhaps you would like a few pears
to take home with you, if they wouldn't be a
trouble to carry?"

"By no means," smiled Acts, graciously;
"pears are a weakness of mine. I should be
very grateful for two or three."

"Go and get some then," said Aunt Rachel,
turning to Tryphena—"some of the golden
sort, and a William or so; take the little

basket and fill it. That'll be handier than
putting them in your pocket. A weight is
apt to tear the linings."

Thus bidden, Tryphena forthwith departed.

"You can let me have the basket when you
come over again," went on Aunt Rachel as the
door closed.

"Yes," said Mr. Latchet, walking to the
window; "on Sunday. How the days shorten.
It is scarcely more than a quarter past four,
and yet you see the sky out there"—pointing to the west—"is already tinged with
red."

"Yes," replied Aunt Rachel, "and the air
feels quite frosty. I'm glad, for my part. I
like the seasons to keep in their places, and
be as they were meant to be. It's your green
Christmases and wet Whitsuntides that make
full churchyards."

The minister laughed, and clasped his hands
behind him.

"You might just as well stay and have a
cup of tea," she continued, unpinning her
shawl; "it wouldn't take five minutes to get
ready—the kettle is on the fire."

"No, thank you," he answered, quickly;

" you are very kind, but I have much work to do to-night. I have been asked to preach at the opening of a chapel in Lyme, and I must consider my subject. I find that town congregations are more fastidious in their tastes than rural; and it is well to be as effective as lies in one's power for the Word's sake. Ah, there is Miss Tryphena"—as she crossed the lawn, the basket in one hand, a pair of garden scissors in the other—" laden with good gifts, as usual, and full of good intentions. I must go to her, or she'll leave you without one blossom."

" We haven't many as it is," was the preoccupied rejoinder; " the gales last week knocked 'em about so."

Taking his hat and stick, Acts hastened to the scene of slaughter.

" Pray don't be so lavish!" exclaimed he, laying a protesting hand on the girl's round arm, " I am not worthy of such excessive liberality!"

" It's no use letting them be beaten to bits by the rain," replied she, placidly, adding a bunch of scarlet geraniums to the marigolds and stocks and mignonette and fuchsias she had already gathered. "The asters are quite done for, you see, and so are the dahlias. Stay —you will have a bit of sweetbrier, that is always worth picking; only you mustn't put it in the same dish with the other flowers, because it kills them."

"Like you, it charms to slay!" he smiled, taking the flowers from her.

She laughed and turned away her head. The minister was fond of trying to seem foolish, just as though he sometimes sickened of his own cleverness.

Slowly they strolled on to the gate.

"This is strange of father, isn't it?" observed she, suddenly coming to a standstill, and shading her eyes with her hand—the sun still had some power.

"Yes," answered he, "it is; but I shouldn't think too much of it, if I were you."

"But," continued she, diffidently, "if he does mean to help the missionaries it is very good of him, is it not? One should be glad of that."

"Yes," he answered again; "without a doubt."

"But do you think he does?" she inquired,

anxiously. "Has he ever said anything to you about it ?"

"Well, no," replied Acts, scrutinizing his boots, "I can't say that he has; I only infer as much from my knowledge of his character —and—general aspirations."

"I am so afraid aunt and he will quarrel over it," said the girl, sadly. "He can't bear to be interfered with—and—"

"We must implore the divine assistance," interposed Mr. Latchet; "with God all things are possible—even the direction of a maiden's choice."

Tryphena's eyes grew puzzled—again she waxed meditative.

"I will add my prayers to yours," he went on; "together we will entreat the Lord. Would that it were side by side. Farewell !"

"Good-bye," she answered, and shook hands with him.

Here a loud tapping at the parlour window attracted their attention.

"Oh!" exclaimed Tryphena, "it's the kettle. I'd forgotten all about it."

"Tryphena!" called Miss Fowke, throwing

up the sash, "how you are wasting the minister's time, and you know he said he was in a hurry."

"It doesn't matter in the least," protested he, stooping down to unfasten the latch, which worked stiffly, "pray don't think of that;" but he spoke to himself—Tryphena was already in the porch.

"I thought the kettle had boiled over," she remarked as she shut the hall-door; "it hasn't, has it?"

"Not to my knowledge," responded Aunt Rachel dryly, with the air of one who suffered.

"I was talking about father, about this ship," continued the girl, cheerfully—"that is how I came to be so long."

"It is no business of yours," was the cold rejoinder; "the idea of a chit like you presuming to mix and meddle. I think I never heard of such impudence!"

"I am eighteen," replied Tryphena, "and I have got my senses as well as other people. If you did not wish me to hear what was said, you should have sent me out of the room."

"I'll take care, pretty good care, to send you out of the room another time," exclaimed Aunt Rachel—"of that you may be very sure. You're getting a deal too forward, ogling and grinning and gracious knows what. Those were not the ways of respectable young women in my day."

"Ogling and grinning!" echoed Tryphena, aggrievedly, "whom have I ogled, and at whom have I grinned?"

"Such impertinence!" ejaculated Miss Fowke wrathfully, and turned to go up-stairs.

CHAPTER XIII.

"THE GOODNESS OF A MAN SHALL PERISH; IT SHALL BE ONE THING WITH HIS SIN."

N crept the one-coloured morns and eves. Sunday came and went in its usual quiet fashion, bringing with it some sunshine and some rain, much peaceful pleasure, and the minister; Monday dawned bright and business-like; Tuesday stark and cold, and yet Mr. Fowke did not come home. He had never been away so long before since he went up to London to see Lord Nelson's funeral, and every hour of his absence seemed to deepen the lines on Aunt Rachel's forehead, and sharpen the tones of her never too sweet voice. She made no remark, however, either to Tryphena or any one else, neither did she invite comment, telling Martha

Tapp to " look to her wash-tub and let be her betters," when that young woman ventured to observe, as she soaped a dimity vallance on Monday morning, that it would " soon be a week since the maister went away." It was not her custom to say much of the thing of which she thought most.

Tryphena shared this peculiarity. Indeed, it was generally held that the Fowkes were a " silent lot;" but with the exception of occasional regrets and movements of contrition, caused partly by a sense of her own demerits and partly by the inequalities of her heavenward path—and every now and then a pang of mental hunger, of impatience at the unwillingness of fact to pair with fancy—her reflections, though sober, were by no means gloomy. Nay, I am of opinion that when free to indulge in uninterrupted meditation, and secure from the chilling influence of blame, she was happier than she had been for long—since Acts first came to Coatham in fact.

For, in the revelation which was to Aunt Rachel as the nucleus of a cloud whence might proceed death-dealing lightnings and fierce ruinous rain, she found a window whereat her

soul might sit and gaze forth on things fair
and new, spotless, fresh from the hand of God
—might bask in sunshine such as fed fruit in
Paradise.

From the hour in which it had first dawned
upon her how mighty is the majesty of pain,
she had yearned to share in those sufferings
whence humanity draws strength, as the live
tree from fallen leaves ; to spend her life in
the service of others—not the service of their
bodies, that anybody could do, but of their
souls ; to lead thousands to the Lord ; to fill
strange lands with the music of His name, to
run out a good course with joy, and then to
die as the marytrs died, triumphant over
agony, proclaiming God's greatness with one's
latest breath, beholding the heavens open
before one's closing eyes — yea, that were
rarely blessed.

And in that square-rigged barque lately
anchored in Bridport harbour, now at the
mercy of Atlantic winds and waves, she beheld
the means whereby she might attain unto the
fulfilment of her hopes. That she would
encounter opposition was certain. No one
ever yet effected any great or lasting good

without having to bear with contradiction,
and the assaults of Satan. Indeed, it would
be a fit subject for regret were it otherwise,
endurance in its way being as useful as effort;
but her purpose being a just one, and in accordance with the commands of Christ, it must
win acceptance in the end; besides, the
minister would side with her—he would add
his prayers, his persuasions to hers. She was
not much wanted at home. She could do very
little good in England, and in Guinea—truly,
the matter admitted not of doubt.

Thus you will perceive that, making due
allowance for the transcendental tendencies of
strong devotional feeling, combined with a
lively imagination, my opinion recently expressed—namely, that when alone, this peculiarly constituted young woman was, despite
her aunt's continued coldness, and her father's
mysterious absence, happier than she had
been for long, is not wholly groundless, but
founded rather on the adamantine basis of
reality.

She possessed also one other incentive to
agreeable thought. On Monday morning, just
as she was about to hang out certain portions

of white bed furniture on a line in the garden, singing softly the while, and, it may be, wondering what Mr. Valoynes might be about, and if he had found his portmanteau at the Exeter coach office—who should come limping up the lane but Isaac the old postman, his bag over his shoulder and a letter in his hand.

"Not for me, Isaac?" smiled she, hastening to the gate.

"Nay," answered Isaac — "'tis for the missus," and therewith he gave it to her.

Tryphena's face sobered. She had seen that handwriting before.

"How odd," said she, "and I was just thinking of him." Then she bade Isaac good-day, and took it into the house.

"My!" exclaimed Martha, who was seated at the kitchen table eating bread and cheese, "what's that—a love-letter?"

"If it is, it's for aunt," was the demure reply. "Where is she?"

"Here I am," called that lady from the scullery; "what do you want now?"

"I've got a letter for you," responded Tryphena—"a letter from Mr. Valoynes."

" Bring it here !" commanded Miss Fowke, and accordingly it was brought.

" Open it and see what he says," pursued she, when Tryphena had laid it on the window-sill, as being the only dry place noticeable, " I've no time for such rubbish."

So Tryphena opened it.

" And there's one for me," said she, as a three-cornered note, inscribed " Miss Try-phena," fell out upon the floor ; " fancy that."

" Ay, fancy !" echoed Aunt Rachel, sourly.

" And he's got to Exeter "—rapidly scan-ning the first page—" and the portmanteau arrived there the very same day, and——"

But her exposition was suddenly cut short. Miss Fowke snatched the letter out of her hand.

" Pshaw !" ejaculated she ; "if you can't read it as you ought, leave it alone."

" But I hadn't begun to read it," expostu-lated Tryphena, red with perturbation; "I was only just——"

" Only just !" mocked Aunt Rachel. " Only just. You ' only just ' yourself back to them curtains, if you please, and take your trash along with you," indicating with her foot the fallen note. "I want no fine stage-madams here."

"But wouldn't you like to see it?" inquired the girl meekly, picking it up.

Aunt Rachel pounced on a gray-ribbed stocking which she had missed this ten minutes.

"If I do, I can," replied she grimly, casting the offending unit into a tubful of hot water, and Tryphena returned to her lines and clothes-pegs. It was at such times as these, when the sunshine of natural gladness mingled so oddly with the raindrops of mortification, that the native fascinations of African deserts became most apparent. Still, although set inharmoniously—this Dorsetshire farmer's daughter had a quite curiously keen sense of congruity; on a fine day, for instance, she would, if she could, have all things fine, tempers, actions, everything save clothes; on a wet day it pleased her to be low voiced, attired soberly;— though set inharmoniously — the fact that Mr. Valoynes had been at the trouble to write to her, had not quite forgotten her in a whole week of new impressions, remained

as tuneful, as pleasureful as it was in it to be,
by right of rightness.

She did not approve of his opinions, regarding them and his general way of thought with
a certain awe and sense of personal danger, as
might a fixed star be supposed to regard the
movements of a comet which had suddenly
obtruded on its privacy, but—and here, too,
the parallel holds good—if he was terrific,
out of all proportion with one's receptive
faculty, increased warmth and light accrued
from his vicinity. When the atmosphere was
no longer rendered luminous by his presence
day became duller, night less visible—thus for
one's loneliness to be irradiated by but one
ruddy gleam, must be accounted a distinctly
joyful occurrence, and so she did account it.

But the gleam was sadly small.

"Dear me!" sighed Tryphena to herself
that night, as having read through her note,
which had throughout the day resided in undisturbed seclusion in the uttermost depths of
her pocket—"why, it seems all beginning and
end, and no middle at all." And then she
read it through again, the silly!

"My dear Tryphena," wrote Robert, "half

14—2

an hour ago I fancied I should never be able to tell you all my news, and now I seem to have no news at all, for that I have missed you more and more every day that I have been away can scarcely be called news. You must know that already. The scenery through which I have passed was very beautiful. Had you been with me I should have pronounced it enchanting. As it was, my eyes did their work but languidly, they would so much sooner have been at the Grange. How grave you will look when you read this! I can see you now; and would say more, if only to provoke that exquisite mouth to a deprecatory smile, did I not fear a cool greeting on my return, which will take place at the very earliest opportunity, be sure.

"For details of my journey and subsequent plans, I must refer you to the letter I have written to Miss Fowke. And now good-bye, with my sincere regards.—Believe me always yours quite faithfully,

"ROBERT VALOYNES.

"If you will favour me with a few lines, please address Post-office, Torquay. I shall be there in the course of a few days."

But Tryphena shook her head. Five minutes ago she thought it not quite impossible
that she might so favour him; but now—she
shook her head again. It is wonderful how
words will change colour when subjected to
lengthened scrutiny. Still it was kind of him
to write, specially after she had refused to
accept that pretty locket he had bought for
her. It was like him. Of course she did not
believe that he had missed her, any more
than that her mouth was exquisite. That
was only a fine gentleman's way of saying " I
am obliged to you for having sewn buttons on
my shirts, and paid attention to the appearance of my neckties ;" like him, too, when one
came to consider. And it was best for persons
to be as God made them, otherwise one ran a
risk of confounding sheep and goats. Yes,
there was really nothing to feel vexed and
get red about. And yet Tryphena hoped
Aunt Rachel wouldn't ask to see it. Why?
Because it was so stupid—that was all.

I think it was about four o'clock on Wednesday, just as Martha deposited her milk-
cans with a rousing clang on the dairy floor,
and the air thickened with the coming frost,

and the smoke as it rose skyward from rubbish heap and chimney took a bluer tinge, that the sound of a horse's hoofs in the road announced to Miss Fowke, who was goffering tuckers at the round table by the kitchen fire, that at last suspense had embraced certainty—that at last the master had returned.

Tryphena was out. She had gone to take a pot of black-currant jam to Kezia Bell, the shepherd's wife, who had just fallen sick of a quinsy, and would not be back for another half-hour for certain, Bell's cottage lying right at the other end of the village, near Deadman's Mill, so called because the last miller murdered his wife, and was hung at Dorchester. Aunt Rachel was not sorry that it had chanced so, being of opinion that the less young folks meddled in the concerns of their elders the better, and desiring to " know the rights of it " without further loss of time.

Slowly walked the horse past the garden gate towards the stable. Aunt Rachel gazed sternly at a " heater " she had just thrust into the fire. Where was Tapp? Another ten minutes to wait, she supposed. Such dawdling work !

But in less than ten minutes, in little more than five indeed, Mr. Fowke's large feet came crunching up the path; Mr. Fowke, his whip under his arm, a pistol in either hand, unlatched the door, entered, and resumed supremacy.

"Humph!" ejaculated he, depositing his burdens on the table, burdens at which Aunt Rachel glanced with ill-concealed nervousness; —for years she had not been able to endure well the sight of firearms, owing to her father having one day, when she was a girl, pointed his gun at her in jest, and narrowly escaped shooting her in earnest, his sleeve catching the trigger; "you've got fire enough, at all events."

"Irons won't heat themselves," she answered.

"Where's Tryphena?" he inquired, taking off his hat, and sitting down to unbutton his gaiters.

"In the village."

"Has anybody been whilst I've been away?"

"No one but the butcher and Mr. Latchet —and the postman," after a pause; "I forgot him."

" What did he bring ?"

" A letter from Mr. Valoynes."

Jacob smiled grimly, and rose to his feet.

" I've got something to say," observed
Aunt Rachel, without looking up—"something that had better be said at once."

" Well !" smiled he, expecting to hear that
he must provide himself with another housekeeper, or that Tryphena had been guilty of
some peculiarly heinous enormity, or that Tapp
wanted a " talking to "—he had so often heard
all this before.

" It's come to my ears," pursued she, un-
rolling a frill and speaking in a thin, hard
tone, "how, I don't intend to say, that you've
turned trader, and have lately fitted out a
ship to go to Guinea. Whether this is true or
false you alone can be judge."

Jacob stood silent. He was averse to lying,
partly because of religious scruples, and partly
because he thought it waste of breath.

" What if I have ?" said he at length.

" This," she replied, facing him, eyes
steady, mouth firm ; " that you've been acting
very wrong both by me and Tryphena,
and every one connected with you. And

where you've got the money from, unless
you've taken mine, goodness alone knows."

"You mind your own business!" retorted
he, angrily; "the money was mine. What
is it to you how I chose to invest it? Not
a penny would ever have found its way
into your pocket, that you may be very
sure."

"Neither do I want it to!" was the tearful
answer. "Abuse is, I know, the only reward
I'm ever like to get for all I've done, or all I
shall do. I look for nothing else. But when
I think of Tryphena, poor motherless young
creature, I feel obliged to speak, to lift up my
voice against doings which——"

"S-s!" burst forth Mr. Fowke.

"Ah, you may hiss!" replied Aunt Rachel;
"them who lives longest sees most. I've
seen others besides you led away by the false
representations of gambling rascals, and 1
know how it all ends. Why, didn't young
Tom Scobell blow out his brains within a year
of his marriage, and all because that mine
he'd bought in Wales proved to be a
swindle?"

"Tom Scobell was a fool!"

"That's what you say of everybody; according to you, the world's nothing more nor less nor a big lunatic asylum."

Mr. Fowke bore the imputation with fortitude.

"But that's neither here nor there," pursued she, briskly; "folks are welcome to think what they please for me, so long as they act upright, and don't go against the Scriptures. What I want to know is where the money came from which has victualled that ship, and your object in victualling her—for an object you must have had, that's plain."

"Suppose I don't choose to tell you?" smiled he, coolly.

"Then I'll find out. I'm as well known at the Old Bank as you."

"What if you are? The Old Bank isn't my mind."

"'Twouldn't long keep my custom if it was," was the tart rejoinder; "and I don't know that it will keep my custom as it is. Preaching the Gospel's all very right and proper, and no one can be more desirous for the salvation of both blacks and whites than I am—no one; but there's a limit to everything. We aren't called to preach ourselves into the workhouse."

Mr. Fowke knitted up his brows as if he doubted the veracity of his ears.

"Whites—blacks—workhouse!" echoed he; "what are you talking about?"

"Well," returned she, stoutly, "that's all I can make of it, except slaving, and it isn't likely you'd meddle with that."

Jacob turned to the window. For a while he said nothing, then he exclaimed roughly:

"Who's at the bottom of all this? Whom have I to thank for making all this mischief?"

"Yourself," she answered; "why couldn't you act straightforward? Why couldn't you say, 'Rachel, I have been asked to go shares in a trading voyage to Guinea. Do you advise it—what's your opinion?' Then there would be no mystery, no uncomfortableness. I should know where I am."

"But I don't care two straws about your opinion," he replied slowly; "you must be duller than I've taken you to be, or you'd understand that by this time. I'm master in my own house, mind that—and I do as I

please, and let anybody interfere with me at
their peril," warming to fierceness.

"God'll interfere with you some day,
though," retorted she boldly; "you may defy
me, and set yourself to work all the wickedness you can lay your hand to, and think that
no man shall see you; but there is One that
seeth and judgeth.   I can wait."

Mr. Fowke laughed, and walked towards the
door.

"Wait for what?" demanded he, scornfully
—"till I turn ye neck and crop out of
doors?"

But Aunt Rachel vouchsafed him no answer,
she had caught the sound of young feet in the
garden. Beauty gave a low whine of pleasure,
and getting up stiffly—she felt the touch of
winter already in her old bones, poor hound—
walked to the door.

"Well, Beauty dear," said Tryphena, as she
opened it and entered, her sweet face radiant
with health and the light of pleasant thoughts
—she was so fond of a walk, particularly when
associated with the performance of some little
act of kindness, being of the tenderest nature,
and simple in her likings as a babe—"and

how have you been this fine afternoon ? and —
Oh, father ! is that you ? I am so glad to see
you. I was just hoping you might come back
to-night."

But Jacob paid no heed. In silence he
shook off the hand she had laid upon his arm,
—in silence he strode slowly off upstairs.

" Whatever is the matter ?" inquired she,
turning aghast to Aunt Rachel. " Isn't he
well ?"

" No," replied Aunt Rachel ; " not at all.
Indeed, I doubt whether he will ever be
well again."

" Goodness !" exclaimed Tryphena, her
cheeks as white as her sun bonnet ; " but
what is it ? Shall I tell John to go for the
doctor ?"

" No," again replied Aunt Rachel, turning
away her head ; " the doctor who could cure
him doesn't live hereabouts."

Tryphena's eyes widened.

" You haven't been asking him questions,
have you ?" said she, fearfully.

But Aunt Rachel replied not. She only
buried her face in her hands, and seemed
to wrestle with affliction.

"Dear, dear!" cried the girl, distractedly; "but this is dreadful. What can I do? Aunt," coming to her side, and placing a trembling arm about her waist, "do please to tell me what I can do to make things better."

"Pray," whispered Aunt Rachel, amidst her sobs—"pray."

CHAPTER XIV.

"THUS WENT SHE LOWLY, MAKING A SOFT PRAYER."

T is curious how angular are the movements of the mind, when viewed in their full extent rather than in the detailed form of separate thoughts. For days, reflection will take one road, then suddenly shoot off, whither it is difficult at first to determine, to what end is seldom instantly apparent, the sport of accident, of a chance word or look, dropped, given, it may be, too frequently is, by one of lower instincts than one's self, for the soul is weak of wing, and would ever sooner crawl than fly.

This trite and somewhat dull observation I am led to make by the consideration of Tryphena Fowke's mental condition at this period.

Between the hour wherein she first heard of her
father's connection with the marine interests
of the British nation, and that in which he
resumed the reins of domestic government,
the idea of self-expatriation had filled her
with joy and hope. To dwell among the
children of a tropic clime, to grow familiar
with the strange sights and sounds of savage
life, to persuade Fantees, or Zulus, or Kaffirs
to become Christians, and wear clothes, also
to abstain from cannibalism and polygamy,
with those incidental weaknesses known
among Europeans as indiscriminate slaughter
and rapine, had seemed to her as perfect an
existence as it was possible for one still burdened by corruption to lead. But, whether
by reason of her natural depravity, and in-
ability to maintain a high degree of spiritual
warmth, or the weakening influence of prolonged meditation, which is apt to dilute enthusiasm, I find—little by little, this faith of
hers waxed faint—so faint, indeed, that but
for constant applications of apposite texts,
and appropriate verses from hymns, combined
with diligent reading of the "Missionary
Calendar" and "Robinson Crusoe," which

immortal work had been duly placed at her service by Mr. Latchet, it is possible it might have died out altogether, with other noble aspirations not wholly inconceivable.

And in her need she could obtain no aid, save that whereto I have adverted, which, after all, was not so much aid as encouragement to hold on till aid came. Aunt Rachel, from being a passive hindrance, had now unwittingly—for Tryphena breathed no word of her ambition to any one—become an active. Since Mr. Fowke's return her manner had softened, her face saddened on such wise, that to regard her—being a kinswoman, and one who if occasionally bruised by her corners, still on the whole had cause for gratitude—with feelings other than pitiful, was impossible. She no longer preserved that unbrokenness of outline, that singularity of detail so essential to the correct appreciation of relative distances ; rather did she betray an inclination to flatness, even a willingness to be trampled upon, alike touching and abnormal.

" I don't think you seem quite yourself, aunt !" said Tryphena one morning, when on going into the store-room to get some rice she

surprised that lady in the act of wiping her
eyes over a jar of pickled cabbage, which she
had just taken down from the shelf to dust.
"The work tires you so, and you look so
white, maybe a change might do you good."

But Aunt Rachel shook her head.

"There's but one change that could do me
any good," smiled she faintly, and therewith
reddened, whereat Tryphena marvelled.

"I was thinking of Weymouth," she answered. "I'm sure I could get on alone for
a week or two, if you'd trust me."

"I could trust you fast enough," was the
chastened answer, "and a vast comfort it is
to think that I can—the only comfort I've
got, seemingly."

Tryphena smiled.

"You weren't of that opinion six months
ago," said she, demurely; "I must have im-
proved of late."

"'Twould be a miracle if you hadn't,"
rejoined Aunt Rachel, with a scintillation of
her former spirit, "considering all the pains
that have been taken with you."

Tryphena smiled again.

"I wonder," she remarked, after a pause,

regarding a spoonful of rice with peculiar interest, "whether you'd miss me at all if I went away."

"Eh?" exclaimed Aunt Rachel, looking up quite startled.

"I don't think you would," continued the girl calmly; "indeed I think you would be glad after a bit. You'd have no one to plague you then, and the house would be quieter Besides, if I were doing better somewhere else."

"Better!" echoed Aunt Rachel—"where could you be doing better? Isn't a child's first duty to her parents and them who've brought her up?"

"I don't know," replied Tryphena; "things come differently to different people—and father's got you to take care of him."

"He may have got me now," returned Aunt Rachel, emphasizing "now," "but that doesn't prove he will have me always."

And then Tryphena went away to make the pudding, but her difficulties had not decreased.

It was at this critical and even alarming stage in the conflict between natural affection

and spiritual fervour, a stage similar to that
ten minutes on which Napoleon used to
declare depended the issue of every battle—a
brief, tremendous pause, wherein Right and
Wrong stepped forth to wrestle for the vic-
tory—that after much meditation, and com-
muning with conscience, the advice and
opinion of Mr. Latchet appeared not only desirable but absolutely necessary to the forma-
tion of a defensible decision which should be
final.

" I will ask him to counsel me, I will open
my whole heart to him. It is quite useless
to grope on like this. Of myself I can do
nothing," thought Tryphena, as she rose from
her knees that night, her cheeks wet with
tears, her face troubled with a righteous sorrow, infinitely beautiful. And by two o'clock
on the next day she, dressed in the straight
brown gingham, black and red shawl, and
Tuscan bonnet trimmed with white ribbon,
which she was accustomed to wear on Sundays,
had already started for Coatham — Aunt
Rachel having freely given her assent, being
in need of sundry threads, cottons, needles,
and cap ribbons, specially fitted for the

exercise of feminine discernment, and, moreover, fancying that a liberal dose of fresh
air and sunshine was as likely to disperse
vapours and eradicate " fads " as anything not
purely medicinal.

" If you chance to meet the minister," called
she, as Tryphena gained the road, "you can remember me to him, and say that your father
would like to see him as soon as convenient
about the new stove—what sort it is to be."

" Very well," replied Tryphena, but made no
mention of her intention to intrude upon that
gentleman's privacy. Speech robbed hope of
charm, she thought, much as rough handling
brushed the bloom off fruit. It was a little
matter, but significant.

Quickly she walked along under the garru-
lous trees, which in places had already made
little pools of dead gold on the road. Overhead spread the unclouded sky, blue in the
zenith, shining white where it kissed the pale
stubble and embraced gray hills. Far away,
far as the eye could reach, stretched the vast
woods, deepened with shadow, rounded with
the bright foliage of wide-spreading beeches
and the lovely birch, which shook out her

tresses to the soft wooing of the gentle wind
as might a fair woman, thought Tryphena,
yield her locks captive to the sweet violence
of love. It was wonderfully good to be abroad
to-day. Never had she seen the autumnal
earth to so great advantage. A person of
moderate desires and a grateful turn of mind
might get no small pleasure by taking note
of those bars of sunlight quivering on the
path, of the divers darknesses on stem and
undergrowth; might even hold felled timber
providential, and the stacking of fagots an
occasion for thankfulness. Quickly, happily,
a pleased smile upon her lips, her young soul
a-quiver with vague joy, she walked along.
Do you think that in thus picturing for you
as best may my humble pen this one maiden
among many, I am overstepping the limits of
what is possible? If so, I answer "No!" Tryphena Fowke is no figment of the imagination,
she has lived and moved and had her being
here, in this island, any time this eighteen
hundred years—will live and move and have
her being so long as the Christian religion is
in existence. Women, I think, best realize
the purity, the unworldliness of women.

And as she reached the brow of Kittock Hill, a somewhat steep ascent, which surmounted, brought you at once within sight and a short mile of Coatham, whom should she spy, toiling laboriously towards her, his hands clasped behind him, his eyes bent on the dusty white road, but Mr. Latchet? The sight gave her pleasure. It would be easier to speak to him of this matter which she held so precious, out here among the birds and bees and flowers — scarce bees and still scarcer flowers—than in that dingy little sitting-room of his, with the chance of being overheard by gloomy-browed, brown-wigged Mrs. Forbes, his housekeeper, hovering in the distance, to mar one's periods and paralyze one's tongue. You see, she had taken tea with him—Aunt Rachel poured out the tea—long ago, when he first came to Coatham, and being of a retentive memory, had preserved a tolerably correct impression of his immediate surroundings.

Slowly the distance between them lessened.

Rapt in thought, the minister seemed for a while quite unconscious of her vicinity, then, however, he looked up—startled it may be by the noise of her light feet—and stopped short and smiled, as should smile one who beheld the realization of his dreams.

CHAPTER XV.

"SHE HOLDS MY HEART IN HER SWEET OPEN HANDS."

"HOW do you do?" said he, having partly recovered from his astonishment. Had you asked him that morning whom he was most likely to meet on his way to Shobdon, the Bey of Tunis or Tryphena Fowke, he would have told you the Bey of Tunis, allowing for human incapacity; "this is indeed an unexpected pleasure."

"Yes," she replied, giving him her hand, "at least"—with a blush—"to me. I did intend calling on you. Aunt wished me to tell you that father would like to know more about the stove, and—and I had something to say on my own account."

"Indeed!" said he, still holding her hand; "and what might that be?"

"I can't tell you all at once," she answered, lowering her eyes in loveliest confusion; "it is too grave; but perhaps if we sat down or I walked a little of the way back with you?"

"Certainly," he replied, "whichever you please; you know that my greatest pleasure is found in serving you. Suppose we sit down," glancing at the bank which was dry and grassy; "you should not overtire yourself."

"I do not get tired easily," she smiled, "especially on such a lovely day as this. Oh, you can't think how exquisite the woods looked, all red and yellow, and here and there just a little green, like some grand lady's dress—an Indian queen's, I fancied. You know this is the first time I've been this way since the summer."

"Yes," answered Acts, seating himself beside her—she had sat down while speaking—"yes; I remember you came in with your aunt to shop, and you overtook me as you drove home. Dear me," and he sighed, "how long ago that seems."

"Does it?" said Tryphena, "not to me. I find the days and weeks and months go all

too fast, so fast that I get quite frightened
sometimes lest I should die, having done
nothing but eat and sleep and be—like an
animal."

Mr. Latchet smiled.

"You are too young to talk of death," said
he, gently; "besides, doing is not everything."

"No," she replied, gravely, "I know. We
sow the seed, but God must give the increase.
But He does give it, does He not, when it is
good seed and the sower is in earnest?"

"Undoubtedly," smiled Mr. Latchet.

For a while she sat silent, her eyes fixed on
the lustrous distance which she thought shone
with quite divine radiance, as might the
dwelling-place of seraphs. Then she turned
to him somewhat abruptly and observed:

"I have been much troubled of late."

"Indeed," said he, considering her judicially,
"what about?"

"The exact limits of one's duty to God and
one's duty to one's neighbour."

He did not answer her at once, seeming to
reflect.

"It is a very difficult question," he said, at

length—"very. But what has raised it in your mind?"

"I will tell you," she answered; "indeed, that is what I wish to speak about. You will remember what you said that afternoon you told aunt about the ship—the ship you saw at Bridport?"

"Yes," he returned, looking mystified, "at least I remember repeating what my friend told me."

"Ah!" she smiled; "but you did more than that—you added a suggestion of your own."

"Did I?" said he wonderingly, knitting up his brows; "my memory gets worse and worse."

"You have so much to think of," was the deprecatory reply; "besides, what must seem very small to you is immense to me; however, not to waste your time, you said that it was possible father might be bent on the conversion of the blacks, and not on buying ivory, as people fancied, and this it is which has set me thinking, for I have all my life long wished to do something real for Jesus—something which no one else would do—and if only I could go to Guinea and preach,—no, I do not mean preach," colouring bashfully, " but——"

Here the profound amazement, not to say consternation, visible in the minister's countenance, froze the words upon her lips. She paused, mouth open.

" Yes," he said, noting her scared expression, " you have indeed surprised me ;" and then he too sat silent, made mute by dismay.

" But," rejoined she, in an argumentative tone, when some two or three minutes had elapsed, " though you may feel surprised, you cannot object. It is surely right to care more for the salvation of others than one's own wellbeing—than even for the good opinion of those who are dear to one."

" That," replied the minister, mildly, " is a proposition of some boldness. Still, granting its tenability, and moreover, assuming that my view of Mr. Fowke's conduct is correct—which by no means follows—the ship has sailed."

" She will return."

Acts raised his eyebrows.

" She may, is, I think, the better way of

putting it," said he ; "and even then it is not certain that her next voyage will be to Guinea."

Tryphena's under lip quivered eloquently and her eyes brightened.

"I thought you would encourage me," observed she, with something like a pout, turning away her head, "instead of——"

"Augmenting difficulties, obstinately refusing to close the eye of reason, and courting your profound displeasure," jestingly.

She remained silent. There were times when even Mr. Latchet jarred her sense of fitness, mostly when he tried raillery. He so jarred her now.

But he smiled on.

"Some tasks," pursued he, blandly, "are so far beyond one's strength that it is madness to attempt them."

She looked at him wonderingly.

"For me to lend the weight of my approbation to this scheme of yours comes within this category," he continued; "it is more than I am equal to : I cannot do it. As soon could I pray for perpetual night."

But she shook her head.

"I don't see," said she dully, "what that has to do with it."

"No!" he answered bitterly, a sigh upheaving his great bosom—like many short, large-headed men, his torso might have served a Hercules—"no! I don't suppose you do. It is not likely, that you should. You young, fair creatures seldom evince any very remarkable powers of discernment," and he laughed unmirthfully.

Tryphena's cheeks reddened.

"I may be young," retorted she, with some faint show of spirit, "but I am not fair, and this is not in the least the sort of talk I wanted," well-nigh moved to tears by the barrenness of reality.

Mr. Latchet picked a veitch leaf, and regarded it as if seeking to derive thence some lesson alike forcible and apposite. Tryphena watched him aggrievedly. Suddenly he looked round at her. Their eyes met—hers fell.

"My child," said he softly, laying his hand on hers, "can't you guess why I seem so hard and unsympathetic?"

"No," she replied, in simplest honesty.

"Then I will tell you," he returned, tightening his hold upon her fingers; "it must be told sooner or later. I love you."

For a moment Tryphena experienced no shock from this announcement. It was only natural that he should love her—Christians always did love one another, to the confusion of infidels and worldlings. She loved him. Then, however, aided perhaps by the intensity of his expression, the full sense of those three words sprang up in the light of her understanding, definite, unmistakable, and—Afric's sunny fountains leapt gladlier than before.

Silently she endeavoured to free herself from his detaining clasp, to rise to her feet. It was very terrible, very! That he should love at all as mortals love—being, as it were, set apart from ordinary men, a sweet-smelling sacrifice, and one wherewith God was well pleased—would be a sad falling away from the ideal, and shock to preconceived notions; but that he should love her—a miserable miscreant like her—the slave of self, of sordid appetites, of all evilness.

"Let me go," said she, piteously. "Oh, pray do let me go."

But he held her fast.

"Not till you have given me an answer," smiled he—"not till you have said, 'Acts, I will be your wife.'"

"Then I shall sit here till doomsday," was the resigned rejoinder.

"Why?" he demanded, stung to incredulity.

"Because that I never can say."

"Why?" he demanded again.

But she made him no reply, feeling, it may be, humiliated by her lack of appreciation. She only glanced at her imprisoned hand.

"How long have you been of this way of thinking?" questioned he, at length, dryly, setting her at liberty.

"I have never been of any other," she answered, pulling down her sleeve, which had fallen back during her struggles, thereby showing pearly-tinted flesh—flesh white as milk —whereon Mr. Latchet's keen brown eyes fastened greedily—"that is, such a thing has never entered my head. How could it?"

"Am I then so unutterably odious?" This just a little sadly. Her rejection of his suit had not damped his ardour, had not weakened his hopes, his convictions that some day he should press bridal kisses on those sweet lips; a girl's "No," must be taken for what it was worth. Mr. Latchet knew that well; still her candour pained him. He had always liked to think that she liked him.

"No, no," exclaimed she, quickly, "anything but that! It is that you are so much too good, so infinitely above me, above everybody. Why, I have always looked upon you as I do upon the Bible."

"But that was scarcely wise," he returned, calmly; "I am only a man."

"No," sighed the girl, rising to her feet with some difficulty—her legs felt cramped and stiff, and the world had changed colour since she sat down—"But I always form my own ideas of people."

"Only a man," pursued he, looking up at her with an ironical smile, "like John Tapp, and Jim Goodwin, and Mr. Robert Valoynes."

Her eyes roamed dreamily away down the road, up which were slowly toiling two cows, and a boy armed with a thick ashen stick.

"I do not think you are much like Mr.

Valoynes," returned she, gently, in a tone as expressionless as her face.

He laughed.

"Perhaps if I were you might be kinder?"

Her eyes hardened.

"I do not like to hear you talk like this," said she, with modest dignity not quite unimpressive ; "it does not seem at all becoming, particularly to a girl like me, who can make no answer, either good or bad. I wanted you to advise me in a certain matter, and perhaps to speak to father and Aunt Rachel, but as you will not help me, I must put all my trust in God. Perhaps"—thoughtfully—"this is meant as a rebuke for seeking earthly aid. His ways are manifold."

"They are," exclaimed the minister, springing up as if smitten with a sudden gladness, "and in that reflection I shall find strength and comfort."

She put back a stray bit of hair which had fallen forward on her forehead.

"But I shall not abandon my intention," she rejoined, firmly, "unless something extraordinary should occur—something no one could foresee."

Acts smiled.

"You are a sweet child!" he said caressingly, "and will some day make a sweet wife. Nay, do not frown, I did not say to me; but like all women, you are obstinate."

"There are occasions when it is one's duty to be obstinate," she replied, with fine promptitude; "for instance, when one is tempted to do wrong, or speak against one's conscience. Without some obstinacy good resolutions would never come to anything."

"No," said Mr. Latchet, "that is true;" and then he paused, to ask when the boy and cows had passed—"Do you happen to know whether Miss Fowke has made any mention to your father of what I told her?"

"Yes," answered Tryphena, relieved by the change in his manner and mode of speech—a change sufficiently remarkable if considered in its integrity; "she spoke to him about it the day he came home, and I think he was annoyed, for she cried a good deal when he had gone upstairs. Besides, they have been very short with each other ever since. I want her to go away for a bit, but I don't know whether she will."

Mr. Latchet looked down at his shoes.

" Have you much to do in the town ?" he inquired, still placidly.

" No," she answered, " not now that I have seen you ; but I must make haste all the same, it so soon gets dark."

" Let me come with you. You will find it pleasanter than being alone."

" No, thank you," returned she, quickly ; " you will be late for tea as it is. I told aunt not to wait for me—father so hates the meals being kept about."

" What does that matter ?" smiled Acts tenderly ; " is not the sight of you my best food and drink ?"

" Good-bye," she exclaimed, thrusting out her hand as it were a stick.

He had surely let himself down enough for one day ; she would not have him sink beyond reclaim.

" Ah !" sighed he, squeezing her limp and irresponsive fingers, " the time will come when you will treat me differently."

" I shall never treat you otherwise than as a

friend," she answered stoutly, " but as a friend
I hope to treat you always."

He smiled.

"Good-bye!" said he; "I wish I might
come with you."

But she turned away, and walked swiftly
down the hill. What use was there in
vain repetitions? vain, because addressed
to ears brimful of foolishness. Tryphena
felt more vexed, more inclined to stamp her
foot and grind her teeth, than she had for
years; than she had, indeed, since Aunt
Rachel put Louisa, her last doll, a lady of
angular figure and a wooden cast of countenance, on the fire, as a solemn warning against
idolatry and the setting of the affections on
things below. To a person of delicate, nervous
organization there is nothing more painful
than to suddenly discover faultiness in that
which has been hitherto held most excellent,
to become conscious of flatness in tones lately
pregnant with deepest charm; the foundations
of knowledge seem shaken, the power of
judgment overthrown.

"I could never have believed it of him,"
thought the girl, ruefully, as she trudged on

through the scantily-peopled streets to the
draper's where she must again take up the
coarser threads of life ; " to talk like that when
I asked for advice and help ! It is shocking.
Whom can one trust ?"

CHAPTER XVI.

THE BREAKING OF THE BATTLE.

WHEN Mr. Latchet reached the Grange, or rather the garden gate of that substantial and valuable specimen of domestic architecture in the seventeenth century, the first person he encountered was its owner, Jacob being engaged in the potting of certain geraniums on which he set store. No smile adorned his countenance, however, as on looking up he recognized his visitor; grim and pre-occupied had been his expression anterior to that gentleman's appearance—grim and pre-occupied it remained. But Acts advanced briskly, unabashed.

"Good-day," said he, with pleasant freedom, "you take Time by the forelock!"

"There was a sharp frost last night," was

the hoarse response, "and there'll be another to-night!"

"Ah!" ejaculated Acts, glancing skywards, critically; "it has that kind of look, certainly. But what a lovely day!"

"Well enough," said Jacob, coolly; he supposed Latchet hadn't walked four miles to praise the weather.

"I met Miss Tryphena on my way here," pursued Acts, after a pause, perceiving general conversation to be attended with difficulty, "and she told me that you wished to discuss the stove, which is fortunate, as that was my object in coming over this afternoon."

Jacob picked two stones out of a trowelful of soil and flung them on to the path, but answer he made none.

"The winter promises to be so severe, and November is so close at hand," continued Mr. Latchet, blandly.

"Yes," replied Jacob, straightening himself up, and lifting his hat from his brow—"yes. Perhaps you'd like to step in and see Rachel."

"Thank you, I should," said the minister, wondering whether Miss Fowke would prove the channel of her brother's good intentions, and therewith turned towards the porch.

"The door is open," observed Jacob, still in the same dry, hard tone.

"And here is Miss Fowke," returned Acts, as that lady made her appearance, clad in a dark brown dress of some thick material, whereof the folds stood out stiffly, the sleeves likewise, a dress singularly unbecoming to one of her square shape and pronounced complexion ; a dress which contrasted ill with one brown gingham, straight of cut and skimp skirted, not wholly foreign to these pages.

"Good-afternoon," said she, blithely, as they shook hands; "I don't know why, but I fancied you'd be over soon. Did you meet Tryphena ?"

"Yes," he answered.

"And did she give you my message ?"

"Yes."

"Well, what a wonder ! Not but what she tries to do her best, poor girl, I do believe. Have you spoken to Jacob ?"—in an undertone.

Acts nodded, and gazed hard into the hall.

"You'd like to sit down and rest yourself a

bit before tea," exclaimed Aunt Rachel, seizing
on his meaning with true feminine acuteness ;
" I dare say you're tired, and it'll be ready in
a few minutes."

" Is the cake done ?" inquired Mr. Fowke,
whose ears were the best of servants.

" It will be by the time it's wanted," replied
Aunt Rachel, coldly—let men keep to what
concerned them—and then they—she and the
minister—repaired to the kitchen, New Year's
Day being the sole occasion on which a fire
presumed to smirch the brightness of the parlour grate.

But though happy in his observations, and
cheerful—singularly cheerful, allow me to remark, for a rejected swain—Acts betrayed no
inclination to resume that familiarity of manner
which he had displayed on foregoing and
similar occasions. Rather did he seem anxious
to withdraw a little, warned, perhaps, by the
warmth of his immediate atmosphere.

" You don't seem quite yourself, sir, I think,"
observed Aunt Rachel, rather stiffly, after a
silence of some short duration ; " maybe you
feel the autumn—I do."

" No," was the calm reply ; " not that I am

aware. Indeed, the autumn is my favourite
season—a liking common to most pedestrians,
I fancy."

"Humph!" ejaculated Aunt Rachel; "I
think of all the rheumatics and toothaches flying about—— We must get that stove set up
as soon as possible. It's only right, of course,
that folks should assemble themselves together
to hear what the Lord has to say concerning
'em; but with souls come bodies, and a barn's
never too warm."

"No," said Acts again, "as we found to
our comfort a little while ago. However, as
you say, the stove will soon be a necessity;
and I just now remarked as much to Mr.
Fowke, who referred me to you."

"Referred you to me!" echoed she, looking
round as she opened the oven door; "whatever should I know about it?"

Mr. Latchet shook his head.

"If that isn't Jacob all over," pursued
Aunt Rachel, aggrievedly, sticking a fork into
the apple cake, and transferring it to the table,
where she proceeded to cut it open and insert
divers bits of butter. "I don't like to speak
against one of my own blood, but really——"

"I may have misunderstood him," interposed Acts; "he only suggested that I
should see you; but as he had given me no
answer——"

"To be sure," she rejoined, and set the cake
before the fire.

"I suppose," observed he presently, with
meditative deliberation, stroking Beauty, who
had just crept out from beneath the table,
stimulated by the goodly odour of that appetiz-
ing confection, "that you did not mention my
name in connection with the Bridport discovery?"

"Do you mean about that ship?"

"Yes."

"No," she replied, peering into the tea-
caddy; "he wanted to know who told me,
but I would not say. A promise is a promise
with me. But why do you ask?"

"I thought he seemed a little less friendly
than usual, that was all."

Aunt Rachel dug out a spoonful of best
Souchong as if she found in that proceeding
an opportune vent for superfluous sentiment.

"He's been like that all the week," said she
at length—"scarce a word in his mouth but

just yes and no, and fool or rascal, as the case might be. I'm sure I can't tell what to make of him; but that no good ever came of such sly, unnatural ways is certain."

"You refer to this venture of his?"

But Miss Fowke held her peace. Jacob having made an end of his gardening, was at that moment in the act of crossing the hall, and she had caught the sound of his footsteps.

In silence he walked through the kitchen out to the scullery to wash his hands at the pump; in silence he returned and took his place at the table, whereat were already seated his sister and the minister, inviting the latter by an upward jerk of the chin, not wholly meaningless to those who enjoyed the privilege of his acquaintance, to the enunciation of grace; in silence the meal commenced.

Aunt Rachel, however, was not the woman to refrain from speech, when persuaded thereto by the voice of reason, out of respect for a brother's unnaturalness. The stove would have to be bought, and Mr. Latchet was the proper person to buy it, an adequate sum being placed in his hands for that purpose. But before anything definite could be settled

concerning make, size, and consuming power
—regarding each of which details one might
well be excused for feeling interest and a desire to know—it was needful to determine
what sum would be adequate, viewed in re-
lation to the present high price of iron and
way of living common among shopkeepers.

" Mr. Latchet," commenced she, gravely,
when Jacob had finished his first cut of cake
and sugared his tea to his liking, " tells me
that when he spoke to you just now about the
stove, you referred him to me, which seems
strange, as I am quite ignorant of your wishes
and intentions."

Mr. Fowke smiled.

" That don't signify," observed he, dryly.

" But it does signify," she retorted ; " how
can any decision be come to unless you're
agreeable ? You hold the purse-strings, don't
you ?"

" Ay," smiled he ; " and I mean to hold 'em,
too."

" Well !"—in the tone of one whose patience
ebbs—" but you mean to have a stove ? You
wouldn't have us all perish of cold, or be kept
away from meeting just for the sake of a few
pounds."

"Pounds are easier spent than got," was the laconic answer.

Aunt Rachel shut her lips tight. Did ever man, being new-born, so shamelessly traffic with the powers of darkness?

Acts sat silent, his eyes on his plate. He was not prepared for this sudden indication of portentous change—portentous insomuch as not a few of his personal comforts, not a little of his public usefulness, had hitherto depended —must always depend—on the estimation in which he was held at the Grange, Mr. Fowke being the head of the church in those parts by long-established precedent and force of fitness, monetary and otherwise. When he looked up his eyes met Aunt Rachel's, wistful, full of meaning. There is ever a certain pleasantness in this secret establishment of a common cause with one to whom we, though willing, are bound outwardly by no stronger tie than that of acquaintance or, perchance, nationality. Miss Fowke felt glad that her hourly trials should at last command the respectful pity to which they were fairly entitled. Nay, a faint gleam of triumph shot athwart her mind as she noticed Acts' softened expression. There

were few women who could have borne so much
so well. But even sympathy—sweet sympathy
—is not without its germ of bitterness. To
Jacob, sitting there—a sarcastic smile upon
his lips, his mind overcast by the gloom of
ungenerous thoughts—that look was as a
challenge, an insolent declaration of defiance.

He broke into a low, hard laugh.

Aunt Rachel flushed crimson—even the
minister changed colour.

"What's that for?" exclaimed she, indignantly; "some sour nastiness, I'll be bound!"

Jacob laughed again, and handed her his
teacup.

"It isn't a trifle that'll make you laugh,"
pursued she, with unabated vigour.

"No," replied he coolly, "you're right
there."

Acts pulled out his watch.

"A quarter-past five!" he exclaimed; "I
must be going."

"As you like!" observed his host, with fine
serenity.

"It's not as I like, though!" said Aunt
Rachel; "I should have liked to have talked

things over sensible, and got my mind clear
for the winter.   Frost and snow bide no man's
bidding, however much he may think of himself—neither do prices, and what's to become
of old Betty Gear, and Daniel Kipps, and
more besides them, if no provision's made for
flannel and warm clothes, with maybe a bowl
of soup once or twice a week, or a bit of
meat——"

" Pooh !"   ejaculated   Jacob,   scornfully,
" there's the union—let 'em go there.   Where's
the use of cossetting up a pack of helpless old
critters, who should be minding their souls
more than their bellies ?   If folks want to be
converted, converted they can be, full or
empty.   Fire and victuals 'll never save a
man."

" Nobody ever said they would," came the
prompt response, " not being a born fool ; but
the Lord Himself has bidden us have a care for
the poor and sick, and them who are afflicted.
He was no stony-hearted tyrant, quenching
the smouldering flax and "—with a slightly-
weakened intonation—" wounding folks' feelings right and left."

" He wounded the feelings of them Pharisees and Sadducees pretty deep, I reckon," remarked Jacob.

Mr. Latchet rose from the table.

" I think," observed he, quietly, " that Miss Fowke's view is perhaps the better of the two, crippled and burdened as is the spirit during its earthly experience by corporeal necessities. Still, if you find that your present charities are a trouble rather than a pleasure, I, in the name of Him I serve, believing in His power to send help when needed, can but say,— withdraw. Now let us pray."

And kneeling down, he prayed that where now reigned darkness might reign light, that that which was crooked might be made straight—so prayed that Aunt Rachel sobbed out loud as she said Amen, and Jacob refused to say Amen at all ; and then, after a brief, meditative pause, stood up and took his hat and bade them each good-night, and went his way gravely, not altogether without dignity, plain, awkward-figured, unancestral, dependent, dissenting parson as he was.

For there is a dignity of spirit as well as of body, and that Acts possessed this dignity which is more intellectual than moral, no one who ever spent half an hour in his society could venture to doubt.

As he turned into the high road he met Tryphena.

" Good-night," he said, seeing that she was about to pass him without speaking.

" Oh, good-night !" she exclaimed ; " I did not know it was you. I have run nearly all the way, and my eyes are quite dim with tiredness !" and therewith she started to run again, as though dreading further speech.

" Poor child !" murmured he, as he trudged on through the deepening twilight, scarce influenced as yet by moon or stars—" poor child ! I did not mean to have spoken so soon : it was rash, dangerous,—but she tempted me —how she tempted me !"

CHAPTER XVII.

WEARY DAYS.

MR. FOWKE did well to pot his geraniums. On the morrow sprang up a fierce north wind, "sharp as a wolf's tooth," said John Tapp; "fit to bite the nose off your face," asserted Aunt Rachel—a wind laden for quick ears with the cries of albatross and penguin, with the crash of splintering icebergs, the snorting of huge whales— a wind that might have stripped King Olaf of his cloak, have played with the beard of Thor, that did strip the Virginian creeper at the Grange as bare of leaves as a six months' babe of hair, and made the trees brown—so brown that you, not a Briton, would have thought that they had been licked by red-tongued fire, rather than tossed, and danced, and gambolled

with by the pure breath of heaven. And to
this mad, keen wind succeeded a dense fog—
a sea fog, damp with brine—clothing the sad,
starved earth in swathes of smoke-like mist,
which, as you gazed, rolled here and there,
but never quite away.

That day Tryphena's hair came out of curl
—and it curled naturally—and the starch,
Aunt Rachel declared, melted out of Jacob's
collars and neckerchiefs as she ironed them;
a most depressing day. And to this most
depressing day succeeded one of pouring
rain—rain on rising, rain when going to bed;
nor did once the drip-drip from eave and water-
spout cease throughout the night.

Verily, the year had fallen sick at last.

"It is as a woman in travail," thought
Tryphena, when, on the third morning, she
looked forth to see a change she hoped, but
hoped in vain, the sky being still unalter-
ably gray, rain-drops still spangling every
leaf—"and grieves because its hour has
come; but when the child, the good New
Year, is born, then the Old Year will die
quite happily. How wise to make Nature
feminine!"

But I should err were I to represent dis-
comfort at the Grange as purely exterior. Indoors, in the domestic atmosphere, was perceptible an inequality, a frigidity, a humidity,
as deterrent to cheerfulness, as provocative of
frowns and dissatisfaction as ever was north
wind, sea-fog, or rain since the world began.
To use four words where three would adequately define intention, seemed nothing short
of wicked prodigality; to smile was rash, to
laugh impossible. Between the master and
mistress of this solemn household speech
other than monosyllabic there was none.

Tryphena pondered painfully, but in vain,
anent the why and wherefore of the change.
Had the minister revealed her secret, his own
disappointment? Was her self-will the
noisome reservoir of blackness whence origi-
nated these miasmatic vapours? This she
inquired of conscience, being of a critical way
of thinking, and inclined to find fault. But
though conscience declined to give any positive
opinion, having a wide grasp of the subject,
reason set her face firmly against the acceptance of either supposition, on the grounds of
inherent improbability, and that which had

since happened. It was not likely that, being aware of her enormities, Aunt Rachel or her father would abstain from comment more or less forcible. Dignified silence might be the fittest channel for the expression of mutual dissatisfaction on the part of elders, persons whose known graces entitled them to occasional relaxation; but when a weakling stumbled—no; Tryphena shook her head. Mr. Latchet had kept his own counsel, or she must have heard of it. This conviction, however, did not decrease her perplexities.

"Well! you do look dowly, to be sure!" observed Martha Tapp, coming upon her suddenly one morning—it was Guy Faux's day, and sunless, of necessity—as she was scattering grain among the cocks and hens, her eyes fixed on a dapper young bantam as sadly as though she beheld in that sprightly biped the determining cause of every woe. "What 'ave you got to fret about now?"

"I don't know," said Tryphena, shaking out her apron, "nothing more than usual, I suppose;" but her voice faltered, and she bit her lip.

"You should go down to the green and see

the guys," said Martha, cheerily ; " there was quite a fair on as I come by—that 'ud brisk you up a bit; and some on 'em's astonishin' fine, pertickler Bony, with 'is 'orns and tail. They'll burn 'im in the bonfire when it gets dark, and fayther said 'e were full o' crackers. I mean to see that, if I can get done in time. P'r'aps Miss Rachel would let you come too ?"

But Tryphena's face brightened not.

"I don't think so," she replied, dully ; " besides, I shouldn't like to ask."

"Shall I ?" suggested Martha, promptly.

" No," was the dejected answer, " I don't care about it. All the sights in the world can't make wrong right."

" No," said Martha, " neither will pullin' a long face. You want shakin' up, Miss Phenie, that's what you want. Good company, smart clothes, and a fine coach to ride in. I know what I'd do if I was a rich young gentleman."

" Do you?" smiled Tryphena, amused despite herself; " and what might that be ?"

" Why I'd say, 'Miss Tryphena, come, marry me !' And you'd say, ' Very well.' And then I'd carry you away to Lunnun, and

wouldn't I just make you look beautiful! You
should 'ave silks and satins and Indy muslins,
fit for any queen, and a green bonnet with a
quilted crown, and a great white feather, like
young Madam Preter. I see her a-settin' in
the carriage before Kelson's the ironmonger's
last market-day, and thinks I to myself,
'You're wheer some one I loves should be.'"

"Oh, but!" exclaimed Tryphena, clasping
her hands and laughing so that Aunt Rachel
heard her in Mr. Fowke's bedroom, where
she was reviewing certain woollens, and wondered "who she'd got now to gossip with"—
Martha was a rare comforter—"suppose I said
'No,' what would you do then?"

"Go away and drown myself."

"Not you," scoffed Tryphena; "you'd set
about finding somebody fresh to tell stories
to."

"H'm!" meditated Martha; "I might—
there's no sayin'. That men are terrible
deceitful is well known; but somehow, I don't
think 'twould be easy to forget you—you're
so different to other girls."

"I'm a great deal more unhappy."

Miss Tapp frowned, and stared hard at a

black-and-white hen, who pecked slower than
the rest.

"What is it?" inquired she at length;
"can't the maister and Miss Rachel 'it it off'?"

"No," answered Tryphena; "that is—they
—they don't seem quite the thing."

"But they aren't put out with you?"

"Not to my knowledge. But I can't bear
to see Aunt Rachel looking so white and
miserable, and father so—— Well," pausing,
"you know the way he's got when he's not
exactly pleased."

"Ay," smiled Martha, and stooped down
to tighten a shoe-lace.

Jacob was no great favourite of hers, though
held worthy of respect as an employer, and
one good at a bargain.

Tryphena's expression altered; she did not
like that smile.

"You must not fancy, though, that I am
complaining," said she, coldly; "no doubt
everything is for the best."

Martha glanced up at her with eyes full of
ironical amusement.

"You needn't be afraid that I shall tell,"
remarked she, dryly.

Whereat Tryphena blushed, and looked at the palm of her left hand.

"It was not that," she answered, in some confusion, "only—talking does no good."

"I'm not so sure of that," said Martha, straightening herself up ; "theer's been times when my 'eart must have bursted for certain, if I 'adn't tilted the lid as it weer, and let it boil over a bit. Besides, why shouldn't you be open with me when you've got a mind ? Wheer's the good of 'avin' friends if you never make use of 'em ?"

Tryphena smiled—that was not her view of friendship.

Just then a hoarse outcry, as of hurrahs mingled with "Remember, remember, the fifth of November !" smote upon their ears.

"'Ere's the guy !" exclaimed Martha, hastening into the road. "Run and tell your aunt; maybe she'll find 'em some pence, poor fellows."

And Tryphena obeyed, but to small purpose, Miss Fowke being in no mood to encourage levity.

"If your father was in," said she, "'twould be different. He can do as he likes with his own. I'm nobody! Give 'em some cider, indeed! Not I! Let 'em go to the Vicarage."

"Oh, but," argued Tryphena, "Guy Faux wanted to blow up the king and Parliament. It is quite proper to rejoice over his being caught."

"Hip—hip—hurrah!" roared the mob.

"How do you know what's proper?" was the shrill rejoinder; "the idea of your setting up for judge! There's a penny"—extracting one from the depths of a capacious pocket—"take that, and tell 'em to be off this moment, or I'll send for the constable. Guy Faux—much they care about Guy Faux, or Guy anything else, but liquor, and making fools of themselves."

Thus may natural bias—this good woman's dislike of merry-making was only second in vigour to her contemptuous hatred of Papists —override established principle, even in the mind of one "called," led out of Egypt with a strong hand and mighty arm, and moreover gifted with an inborn sense of the worth of conviction.

In this dark and penitential season it would seem only reasonable that a young person of

Tryphena's mental inclinations—a young person whose imagination was apt at the extemporising of shelter, rich in resources—should have turned from the cheerless present to the sunlit future, should have substituted freedom, realized ambition, and a life spent beneath palm-trees, by cool rills, surrounded by the dusky children of a great and unfettered race, for bondage, sickening hope, and the brown ugliness of frost-bitten Britain, not merely with readiness but rapture. And yet her thoughts took not this colouring.

"I am sorry I spoke to the minister," mused she, not once but always, when solitude unchained reflection; "ever since that day my ideas seem to have caught cold. Intentions are like young plants—they must be kept warm and let alone if you want them to grow up strong and healthy. Perhaps it is foolish to feel so; but he is so wise and knows so much. I do wish that I had held my tongue."

Had she been keener-witted, it must, I think, have struck her how subversive of that belief in an overruling Providence which yielded her so great consolation, were these

repinings ; for, according to her creed, that
which was predestined had been predestined
from all eternity, and without predestination
nothing could occur, not even the death of a
sparrow—wherefore the yea or nay of man
possessed but an ideal and relative significance, little better than none at all. But
Tryphena, though meditative, was averse to
analysis, having been duly inspired with
horror of reason, as leading to atheism, a
fondness for Byron's poetry, and contempt
for existing institutions—notably parental
authority—from her earliest years. Mr.
Latchet's arguments, based on matter of fact
and irrefragable, if one must be bound by
natural conditions, vexed her sorely, vexed
her on such wise, indeed, that at length she
felt quite wroth with that stubborn and clear-
sighted gentleman. It was so cruel to crush
zeal beneath the deadweight of experience—
as cruel as to rob an apple-blossom of scent
and loveliness by piling on it musty tomes,
the work of forgotten sages. Unplucked, fed
by the sun and dews and soft spring showers,
that flower would certainly have brought forth
fruit—good, wholesome fruit, fair to the eye

and sweet unto the taste. Tryphena could have wept for mortification—nay, did weep sometimes, when fate was favourable.

But on meeting Acts face to face, constrained partly by the memory of past pleasantness and partly by self-distrust, she maintained her usual friendliness of manner; for no man was faultless—neither should one Christian presume to judge another.

If, however, she thus curbed her natural leanings, Mr. Fowke evinced no such moderation. Ungracious, not to say uncivil, he had shown himself about the stove, and ungracious not to say uncivil he continued.

"If you don't wish the minister to come here," said Aunt Rachel, one Sunday evening, being hurt by Jacob's manner at tea, or rather lack of manner, he never looking off his plate or saying a word he could avoid—"you had better say so. I am sure he is the last man in the world to intrude where he is not wanted, and it can be no pleasure to him to be treated as he was treated to-night."

"By whom?" inquired Jacob, coolly, without taking his pipe from his mouth. They were sitting in the kitchen, Tryphena at the

round table reading the "Pilgrim's Progress."

"By you !"

He laughed.

"I can't think what's come over you of
late," pursued Aunt Rachel, mournfully;
"you're no more like the man you were a
year back than chalk's like cheese."

Tryphena looked up with big, scared eyes.
Was the storm about to burst at last? She
had been dreading an outbreak for days. The
colour faded from her cheeks.

Mr. Fowke maintained a stolid silence.

"See," broke forth Aunt Rachel at length,
"what an interest you used to take in good
things—meeting and the minister's discourses,
and whether the barn was full or empty.
Now you don't seem to care a bit who goes or
who stays away. Indeed, I do believe that if it
wasn't just for shame's sake, and the thought
of what folks would say, you'd stay away
yourself."

"There you're wrong," he answered quietly;
"but I pin my faith to no man. No man
shall ever get the whip hand of me, I promise
him."

"That's all very well," she rejoined; "not that anybody wants to, as far as I am aware, or need, for the matter of that; but you might be civil."

Jacob smoked on, emitting a little cloud of blue smoke from the corner of his long, lean-lipped mouth every now and then, with a small suctional sound as of enjoyment.

"And just consider the chapel," she continued, with increased animation; "six months ago it was to have been begun this summer, the foundations dug, the ground cleared, and I don't know what. Here is November and not a nettle pulled up, and yet you seem quite content."

"There's no hurry," responded Jacob, placidly; "the spring's the best time for building."

"Yes," said Aunt Rachel; "but you say nothing about it—you leave everybody in such suspense. I know the minister's face better than you do, and I can see that he is getting uneasy. Why don't you speak out, and let us know what you're going to do?"

"Because I don't choose," was the deliberate answer; "because the land's mine, and the bricks are mine, and the mortar's mine, and the wood is mine, and I shall have to pay for putting 'em together. If Mr. Latchet can't bide my pleasure, why doesn't he find the money himself?"

"Ah!" exclaimed Aunt Rachel, not without bitterness—"that's where it is: that nasty grudging spirit, always wanting to ride rough-shod over everybody. If I was Mr. Latchet I'd have nothing to do either with you or your land. I'd just go and call on every one I knew and put the case before them, and with what they gave make myself content."

"Suppose they gave nothing?" smiled Jacob, dryly; "Latchet's too wise for that. He knows which side his bread's buttered if ever any man did; you don't catch him with chaff."

To this assertion Aunt Rachel vouchsafed no immediate reply, but the form of her visage indicated that the fire burnt.

"You didn't speak like this always," observed she at length; "there was a time when you saw things like other people, and could honour a good man when you met him."

18—2

"Ay," smiled Jacob, "there was a time when I laid in a cradle and wore petticoats."

"How do you mean?" she questioned, gazing up at him fearfully. Had he turned infidel?

But he only laughed his habitual low sarcastic laugh, and having exhausted his pipe, knocked out the ashes on the hearth, and replaced it on the mantelshelf. That done he sought for his hat. Clearly, conversation had exceeded the narrow limits of the attainable—for the present. Tryphena breathed more freely.

CHAPTER XVIII

STRANGE WEATHERS.

WEEK slipped by—a week of rain and wind and wearisome expectancy. To-day it seemed so likely that to-morrow would be fine—would bring change, fresh cause for interest—so certain was it when to-morrow came that that which had been all too faithfully set forth that now to be ; one got tired of hoping.

Mr. Latchet, though seen at a distance by Tryphena on Thursday afternoon, as cloaked and hooded she made her way through mud and mist to the shop before mentioned, paid no visit to the Grange till the following Sunday, a circumstance which afforded Aunt Rachel occasion for mysterious ejaculation, and looks not wholly devoid of meaning—

looks directed chiefly at Mr. Fowke, though sometimes falling on inanimate objects, such as pin-cushions, loaves of bread, the ceiling, with a happy artlessness and apparent absence of design most praiseworthy.

"What are you staring at now?" inquired Jacob sharply, as he pulled on his riding-boots after dinner on Friday, having caught sight of her pre-occupied face.

"Nothing!" answered she dully; "I was thinking."

And Jacob smiled—smiled and stamped his right foot on the floor forcibly, as though it were alive and could feel pain.

"Get me my gloves," said he to Tryphena; "I'll back doing against thinking any day."

When Sunday came, however, it seemed as though his mood had softened; why, it was difficult to understand, unless you believed in the efficacy of prayer, and the innate inclination towards right of a once-awakened conscience. Aunt Rachel's face waxed exultant as she, having with Tryphena lingered behind after service to say a comfortable word or two to Hannah Beer, who had that day brought

her babies to be christened, saw them, Jacob
and the minister, walk away Grangewards,
deep to all seeming in familiar conversation—
conversation such as it had been their wont to
indulge in prior to that unlucky visit of Acts
to Bridport—conversation whence good could
not but arise.

"See!" said she, delightedly—the twins
being reshawled, and safe in the arms of their
parents—"they've made it up. I thought
they would. Depend on it, 'twas that last
sentence that did it. I must ask Mr. Latchet
to put it down on paper for me. What a
good thing that I baked yesterday. Dear!—
How glad I am, to be sure!"

But Tryphena smiled not, neither did she
reply. It was only natural that a man like
"father" should, in the ripeness of time, give
renewed evidence of grace. That he would
cherish emotions unbeseeming a professor,
was not to be supposed for a second. She
never had entertained any such supposition.
The only thing was, that with him self-revision
seemed a somewhat more lengthy process than
with others probably, because performed in a
superior manner. Nothing here to make an

outcry about—nay, the making of an outcry
was in itself suggestive of past strictures not
altogether favourable.   She held her peace.

" Well, ain't you pleased ?" pursued Aunt
Rachel, aggrievedly ; " I should have thought
you'd have been quite overjoyed—I'm sure
you ought to be."

" I knew father was only a bit put out,"
answered the girl calmly ; "maybe he had
other things to vex him, too ; and I'm sure the
weather's enough to try any one's temper."
—looking over her shoulder to ascertain the
damage, if any, sustained by her petticoat, a
black one, and quilted—during their brief
progress up the lane.   .

" The weather," retorted Aunt Rachel, " is
as the Lord wills it should be.   What's good
enough for Him is good enough for you.   Why
don't you pick your way ?"

" I do," responded Tryphena, " but it is no
use.   I am over shoe-top already."

"Is your patience quite exhausted ?" inquired Acts, suavely, opening the garden gate.

Jacob had gone indoors to see to the kitchen
fire, but he had waited.

It was a week since he had beheld, save in

dreams, the face he found fairest under the sun ; and a week is a weary time considered thus.

"I should think yours must be," replied Aunt Rachel, graciously, tendering a mittened hand, the which he shook with warmth—if the master had money, so had she, and that *aurum* is a neuter substantive every school-boy knows—" standing there in the fog. We were afraid almost that you wouldn't come— it was so gloomy."

Acts smiled.

"So Mr. Fowke tells me," he answered ; "but you should have known better than that," and his eyes sought Tryphena's, which were, however, fixed upon her feet—muddy little feet and cold.

"Well," observed Aunt Rachel, "I did go so far as to say it would be strange if you didn't. But don't let us loiter here, or we shall be down with ague ; there's a deal of that about just now. I dare say you've got it at Coatham."

"Yes," replied Acts, as they moved on towards the house. "At least I know of one case. Mr. Fowke seems better."

Aunt Rachel looked puzzled.

"I thought," pursued he, gently, "that when I saw him last he appeared rather out of spirits—fagged."

"Father has not been exactly himself for some time," observed Tryphena, gravely.

"But he is quite different to-day," rejoined Acts—"quite, and I am glad to see it, for I fancied——"

"You need fancy nothing," interposed Aunt Rachel; "you just go on in your own way, and it'll all come right, mark my words. You've no occasion to fret yourself."

Acts lifted his hat from his head, and gazed away into the twilight, as one tempted by belief, if but chill reason would approve.

Tryphena walked on into the hall. What did Aunt Rachel mean by talking like that? —what could Aunt Rachel mean? Was there ever anything so annoying since the world began?

At tea Mr. Fowke, though inclined to silence, as became one on whose leanings depended the happiness of others, preserved a bland vacuity of countenance, sufficiently en-

couraging. It was a curious trait of this man
that the expression of his face in repose was
distinctly amiable, even smiling, but only in
repose. Directly he spoke the smile vanished,
the amiability likewise.

"Farmer Fowke do be loike my Turk," one
day observed Abraham Charm, erst a shepherd,
now chief raggamuffin, brawler, and ruffian of
that ilk, pointing to his bull-dog; " 'tisn't
till 'e do open 'is mouth that you see 'ow ugly
'e be !"

And Abraham was right.

At tea, however, I repeat, Jacob preserved
that appearance of good temper which had
distinguished him throughout the day, and
conversation flowed briskly, change being, as
we all know—we of this enlightened generation—a potent provocative of intellectual
brilliance. Still he played auditor rather
than actor, till a break having occurred,
owing to the shallowness of the teapot, he
exclaimed, pushing away his plate :

"Yes, we shall soon have him back
now."

"Have who back?" inquired Aunt Rachel,
with a reckless disregard of grammar, the

memory of which fills me with awe—"that'll do, thank you, Mr. Latchet."

"Why, Mr. Valoynes," answered Jacob, rubbing his hands; "Squire Valoynes—Lord Valoynes. Come, now; that doesn't sound bad, eh, Phenie!"

Tryphena looked up in wonder; it was not once in half a year that she thus heard herself addressed, save by the Tapps, who, being simple folks, liked short words better than long ones.

"Dear, dear!" said Aunt Rachel, "what a way to talk. Besides, I thought you didn't hold with titles? Not that all the titles in the world could make a pin's difference to him you're speaking of; king or beggar he'd be just the same."

"Yes," said Tryphena, softly.

"Happy he!" smiled Acts, replacing the kettle on the hearth, and returning to his seat, "lapped in the soft ease of such fond memories. By-the-way, I've been going to ask a dozen times, but something has always intervened, have you heard from him since he left?"

"Yes," said Aunt Rachel. "I had a nice long letter about a fortnight or three weeks ago. He was then at Exeter, and seemed in excellent health and spirits."

"And Phenie heard too," added Jacob, "but she didn't care to show her letter—not she! Ah! it's a queer world!" and he leant back in his chair, and thrust his hands into the pockets of his nankeen breeches, and compressed his lips tellingly.

Tryphena's cheeks crimsoned, and her eyelids fell—large white eyelids, delicately veined as are the petals of the wild flower called wood-sorrel, and fringed with softest brown— beautiful eyelids Robert used to think. Her heart, too, beat quick and hard. She longed to speak, but knew not what to say, loving truth.

"Indeed!" observed the minister, noting her confusion.

"Ay," smiled Jacob,—"'still waters run deep.' There's no saying what may happen some fine day. For my part, I think folks should be let to choose for themselves, so long as the money's all right."

Acts made no answer. Adept as he was in

the control and concealment of feeling, he felt that silence was best eloquence just now.

"That Mr. Valoynes is rich," said Aunt Rachel, "no one can doubt; but riches are not everything. If only his faith was as good as his fortune, I should be the last to object."

"Object to what?" exclaimed Tryphena, facing round, made desperate by shame— it was quite horrible to be talked about in this way, before one's face, with another man sitting by—another man who had all sorts of thoughts in his head—"I can't imagine what you mean; but"—tearfully—"if you keep on I must go upstairs, I must really!"

"Pooh!" scoffed Mr. Fowke; "that's all very fine. Wait till Mr. Valoynes comes back. You'll be pleased enough to see him, I'll warrant."

"So will aunt, so will you, so will Mr. Latchet. Why should I be picked out and made an example of? It is a shame!" with vast indignation.

"Sh!" interposed Aunt Rachel; "you mustn't speak like that, my dear. No one wants to make an example of you or anything of the sort. Your father's only joking."

"Then," said Tryphena, "I don't like such jokes. They are very indelicate and improper!"

"Lord!" ejaculated Jacob; "what'll the women say next, I wonder? That marriage itself is indelicate and improper!"

"I hope not," smiled Acts, dryly; "I should be sorry to be thought to encourage doings liable to be called either one or the other."

Whereat Jacob laughed—laughed and threw back his head, as was his way when tickled by a notion.

Aunt Rachel, however, preserved a decorous stolidity.

"Matrimony," remarked she gravely, "being an ordinance of God, must, fitly entered into, enjoin a blessing; but the choice of a partner is a very grave concern, and one on which too much thought cannot possibly be expended, in my opinion."

"An opinion," observed Acts, "in favour with most ladies, to judge from results."

"Ha, ha!" laughed Jacob—"that's not bad, that's not bad at all! I dare say, now, you find 'em rather troublesome over at Coatham—got to keep 'em under—let 'em feel you're not to be trifled with?"

"No," said Acts, placidly; "I cannot say that I'm an object of much attention."

"Not handsome enough, perhaps," smiled Jacob; "it's your handsome men that have such a time of it—men like Mr. Valoynes, now. I'll bet a crown to sixpence that he leaves wet eyes behind him wherever he goes."

"Dear me!" interposed Aunt Rachel, somewhat pettishly, "you're mighty fond of Mr. Valoynes all of a sudden. Three weeks ago he was everything that was bad. It was as much as I dared do to mention his name, and now, as poor mother used to say, he's the tenth wonder of the world."

"Ay," said Jacob; "better late than never. I don't see things quite so quick as you clever young people."

And then he got up, and going to the hearth, invited the minister to come and warm himself a bit before he started, for it was a desperate cold night ; and Acts accepted the invitation—in silence, though,— lacking not food for thought.

CHAPTER XIX.

FROM WAVE TO BEACH.

ONDAY dawned red but dry—the wind having changed, and a slight frost set in during the night. Mr. Latchet felt a difference in the air as he walked home, a difference akin to that noticeable in his reflections when compared with those wherewith he had beguiled his midday leisure ; for Mr. Fowke's sudden and extraordinary reversal of opinion concerning Robert Valoynes, his remarks anent still waters, the charms of wealth, and last, but in nowise least, that letter received and doubtless treasured by Tryphena, coupled with her obvious confusion at its mention, and Aunt Rachel's indifference—not to say blindness—made him feel seriously uneasy. That Jacob, who, for

all his narrow-mindedness, was a man of con-
siderable sagacity—vulpine it is true, and of
little service beyond the limited radius of his
own experience, but sagacity nevertheless—
that Jacob saw farther below the surface of
things than he chose to show, was very likely.

" He has already guessed or discovered the
nature of my desires, I have no doubt,"
thought the minister, " but that is no reason
why he should further them." The popular
voice might proclaim Shobdon Grange happy
in its master, might dwell upon his graces,
might enumerate his virtues as loudly as it
pleased, but the popular voice had little weight
with Acts Latchet. He listened smilingly to
its assertions, occasionally fell in with its de-
cisions, oftener remained neutral, always made
mental reservations, which to a candid and
simple-minded person might have seemed
inimical to the correct expression of belief
under any circumstances whatever. Specially
did this doubleness of vision affect his estimate
of character, human character, the inclinations
and intentions of the men and women among
whom he dwelt, and by the culture of whose
spiritual affinities he made a living. To the

19—2

world at large—that is, the small dissenting
world of Coatham, Chadlington, Liss, and certain other centres of rural industry—the Fowke
family presented a spectacle alike uncommon
and delightful. "Head, heart, and hands,"
remarked Mrs. Fleming, the wife of the chief
grocer at Chadlington, and a leader of opinion,
to Acts one day, "knit together by natural
affection and Christian piety. I took tea
with them last week—and came away thinking that I had seen no sweeter sight since I
stood by the death-bed of poor Mrs. Tucker,
the mother of ten and dead in three days. It
is no wonder that he makes money."

And Acts replied gravely, "No, indeed!"

But he had his own opinion all the same,
peculiarly his own.

Jacob Fowke was, according to him, when
exposed to the searching light of pure reason,
not so much a Christian as a hypocrite—more
of a tyrant than a saint, a trader to the
slenderest ramification of his nature, and of
the worst type, willing to make good
his stalking-horse, God his shield. A smile
would flicker on the minister's lips as he
glanced from the one picture to the other.

There is as much amusement as profit to be derived from the making of just comparisons.

Thus, disguise being rendered ineffectual, and the man known as he was, thoroughly well appreciated and enjoyed, that he should suddenly let go old prejudices, and devour his own words uttered at no very recent date, might well move one given to weigh statements—and moreover possessed of a direct interest in the meaning of the change—to reflection.

Acts felt uneasy.

Monday, as I have already said, dawned red, but dry, neither did it rain all day; still, it was dull, the sun appearing only at intervals, as a candescent globe in the midst of fiery clouds—clouds which John Tapp declared foretold more wet, to Tryphena's great dissatisfaction; for John was a prophet of renown in his own country, and justified his fame, which is more than can be affirmed of certain other great men of my acquaintance. On this occasion, however, his prediction fell short of fulfilment, for by the following morning, grass, shrubs, and ground, bare branches, twigs, and thatch were powdered with hoar frost, thin

ice made of each pool a solar looking-glass;
the dead leaves cracked crisp beneath one's
tread; over the brown hills, the yellow woods,
hung that luminous haze so true a presage of
fair noons; the birds chirped and quarrelled
and flitted to and fro from roof to ivy bush,
from ivybush to wall, from wall to roof again,
in busiest idleness; a robin—the first robin—
perched on the scullery window-sill, and winked
its bright eyes at Tryphena as she washed up
the breakfast-things, so audaciously, that had
she been a student of Hellenic philosophy, she
might have reverted to the doctrine of
metempsychosis, and imagined that plump
brown body the last refuge of some gay love-
locked cavalier :—clearly the weather would
take up at last.

"Dear! I am so glad!" exclaimed the
girl, her eyes fixed on the clear sky, a bright
smile upon her lips; "I can hardly stand still
for happiness, though why, I'm sure I don't
know!"

The robin remarked "cheep."

"Nor any one else, I should say!" exclaimed
Aunt Rachel, from the kitchen.

"I think it is because it's fine," pursued

Tryphena; " I always feel pleasant when the sun shines. Don't you ?"

" No," was the sober answer; " I like shade. When it's all so bright, things seem to lose their meaning."

" Do they ?" said Phenie. " Not to me."

" Besides," continued Aunt Rachel, appearing with a flowerpot in each hand—she had been seeing to her plants, in which she took much pride and pleasure—" one must be quite at ease to enter into gaiety ; which being a Christian is impossible—here below, at least."

Tryphena's face waxed grave.

" And yet," said she, thoughtfully, " it is scarcely likely that the earth has been made so beautiful just to tempt one to do wrong."

Aunt Rachel shook her head.

" Beauty's oftener a curse than a blessing," observed she — " it leads a many into sin, who but for it would have died happy."

" Ah, that sort of beauty, yes !" replied Tryphena, promptly ; " but I wasn't talking of that—it was of the trees, and fields, and sky, and creatures — that I was thinking. Look at that robin now — what could be prettier !"

" A robin !" exclaimed Aunt Rachel, looking round—" where !"

" On the window-sill."

" So there is—well, to be sure ! We shall have snow soon."

" Oh !" exclaimed Tryphena, petulantly, "you *are* in a gloomy mood. Even the poor robin must mean mischief."

And a frown puckered up her forehead.

Was one never to get further than implacable vengeance and inborn fellowship with Satan ?

Aunt Rachel smiled.

" If you could have your way," remarked she calmly, " life would be nothing but a fair."

" As well that as a funeral," was the tart retort ; " besides it isn't true."

" Eh ?" said Aunt Rachel.

But Tryphena reiterated not her indiscretion ; she took refuge in a glass-cloth. It is wonderful how great is the sheltering capacity of most objects rightly approached. After all, the sun hid his face at no man's bidding, not even an aunt's ; neither did the birds curtail one

chirp, nor the gold and ruby chrysanthemums
fold a petal. The robin, it is true, flew away,
but that was owing to baulked hopes—hopes
not wholly unalimentary—in nowise consequent on eavesdropping. It will be perceived
that Miss Fowke, junior, was scarcely in so
proper a frame of mind as she might have
been this fine November morning.

The clock had just struck eleven, and the
quilted blue-and-white counterpane—quilted
by Rebecca, sister to Tobias, born May the
tenth, seventeen hundred and seven, died un-
married January the tenth, seventeen hundred
and seventy—had just been spread on Jacob's
bed, when some one knocked loudly at the
back door.

" I'll go," said Tryphena, who had by this
time quite recovered her equanimity, as
became a young woman of principle ; " it'll be
Isaac."

And therewith she hurried from the room.

Aunt Rachel walked to the window—she
did not approve of idle expectancy, neither
had she anything to expect in particular, only
it was about the time that Mr. Valoynes had
fixed for his return, and——

" See !" cried Tryphena, bursting in upon
her relative's reflections—" like a rat in a hen-
coop," thought her relative—" here's a letter
for you ; and may I give Isaac a bit of bread
and cheese ?—he does seem so pinched."

" Very well," said Aunt Rachel, regarding
the document in question with eyes grave and
a little doubtful ; "but cut from the old cheese.
What a scrawl, to be sure !"

" Perhaps he was in a hurry !" suggested
Miss Bountiful.

Then Aunt Rachel tore open the letter,
returned to the window, and commenced its
perusal ; but no little three-cornered note
tumbled out this time, Mr. Valoynes had been
single enough of intention this time. Slowly,
even a little sadly, it is depressing to discover
error in one's estimate of a person, be that
estimate high or low—the girl turned towards
the door.

" Well," exclaimed her aunt, looking up—
" what are you waiting for ?"

" Nothing !" and a faint reddening of the
cheeks.

" Then you'd better make haste."

And Tryphena obeyed—obeyed with a

heightened colour, and an odd brilliance in
her eyes ; with a hurt heart in her bosom, and
a proud resolve in her mind.   Isaac would be
glad of his bread and cheese, no doubt—it was
a good thing that Isaacs would never perish
out of the land—but it was very unkind of
him not to write to her—very.   How could
he suppose that she would ever so far forget
herself as to write to him ?—that was absurd
—out of the question altogether.   He was
very unkind—not that she cared about it, not
in the least—of course not.

And yet the blue sky had of a sudden lost
its blueness, the sun his sunniness ; the birds
chirped not, neither did the ice sparkle ; and
the robin—horrid robin—Aunt Rachel was
quite right to call him the precursor of misfortune.   And all this wreck of nature because
one young man had forgotten or did not care
to write to one young woman.   *Eheu !*

But it was not kind of him.

If Miss Fowke guessed the cause of her
niece's altered manner—the girl resuming her
work languidly, as if it were a load to be
panted under rather than a support to be leant
on, all the joy expressed from face and voice

—she said nothing to betray her knowledge, deferring all reference to Robert's letter till dinner time, when—the restorative process being well commenced—she informed Jacob that Mr. Valoynes was coming back on Thursday.

"Indeed," said Jacob, and took a long pull at his mug of cider.

"He might," pursued she, "have written a bit sooner, I think, but I suppose he couldn't quite make up his mind; and after all it doesn't much matter—for the room is ready."

"Yes," replied Jacob, "yes. Did he write to you?" this, turning to Tryphena, who, pale and subdued, was gazing down at Beauty, as usual stationed by her side, with eyes full of grave affection.

"No," she answered, without looking up.

"Nor send any message?"

"He begged to be kindly remembered," said Aunt Rachel, coldly.

"Humph!" grunted Jacob. "Well," opening his snuff-box, "he can come—I've no objection to that."

"Wonders will never cease," smiled Aunt Rachel, sarcastically.

But he made her no answer.

The shaft must be sharp-tipped, indeed, that could pierce the thick plates of his egoism.

To Tryphena this intelligence—intelligence which had of late ranged itself under the head of things desirable, for it was certainly pleasant to have some one to walk with and talk to and occasionally feel sorry for, some one fresh and good-tempered, and fairly quick-witted— to Tryphena, I say, the news of Robert's projected reappearance scarcely conveyed that sense of satisfaction she had anticipated. Perhaps she might see more in it to-morrow— anything really good was sure to be known as such sooner or later; but somehow the world had changed since he went away—and for the worse. It was so much colder, there was not a flower to be seen, except the chrysanthemums, and they had been so cut by that bitter north wind, poor things, that not one bud in six dared to open, and father, up till last Sunday, had seemed so strange ; even Mr. Latchet had shown signs of weakness, of, if one might be forgiven the expression, backsliding, alike saddening and calculated to alarm. No, she was of a surety less glad than she had expected to be.

Still her reflections were not whole-tinted. What reflections ever were? It would have been distinctly disappointing if Mr. Valoynes had gone straight back to Kirton (she knew a great deal about Kirton, between you and I, was intimately acquainted with its aspects exterior and interior, having been there often in dreams day and night) without turning aside to say good-bye. He would not stay long, Christmas being already within hail. That would be matter of regret to no one, but it would be nice just to have a parting glimpse of him before he vanished finally into the chill realm of memory. Yes, looking forward it was possible to be not merely resigned, but mildly cheerful; looking back or sideways tended to depression, it was true. There was, however, no particular reason why one should look either back or sideways. Nay, such looking savoured of ingratitude and self-will. If only father wasn't so fond of making fun of people, if only one could feel sure of what he might do or say. Fancy, now, if he were to begin his jokes before——

"Why, Miss Phenie," exclaimed Martha, looking up from a gown body on which she was hard at work—being a clever needle-woman, she was sometimes requested to assist in the family dressmaking—and fixing her little red brown eyes on the girl's pink face, "whatever can you be a-thinkin' of? Nothin' bad, I 'ope."

"No," said Tryphena, with a pin between her teeth, she was at work too; Aunt Rachel wanted to wear that gown, a green satinet, on the morrow:—green was her favourite colour, after blue.

"Then what set you blushin' so? A minute ago you was as white as that linin', and now you're as red as a flame. Give me them scissors."

"I was wondering!" replied Tryphena, gravely.

"Ah!" said Martha, enlarging an armhole, "but what about? Not that you need trouble to say. I've got eyes in my head, and sense too; nobody need make two words of one for me."

"You've got a good opinion of yourself, anyway!" remarked Tryphena, dryly.

"To be sure I have!" was the prompt rejoinder; "why shouldn't I? A clever body's a clever body, and a fool's a fool. Nothing can alter that, more than it can pretty and plain. For instance—there's you and Mr. Valoynes, you're handsome; and there's me and the minister—we're ugly, ugly as sin, and all the soft sawder in the world won't better us."

"Oh, but," said Tryphena, "I don't call Mr. Latchet plain—he has such fine eyes and so sweet a smile."

"When 'e smiles at you," rejoined Martha; "'tain't so sweet to every one: ask fayther!"

Tryphena held her peace. That John was scarcely so hot in the pursuit of righteousness as might have been expected in one of his probity and antecedents was no secret; neither that Acts had before now ventured on private rebuke, finding public exhortation of no effect.

"It is a pity to give cause for offence," observed she at length; "but a minister is justified in speaking—when he thinks it needful."

"Ay!" replied Martha; "ministers do seem to me to be justified in doin' most things as they've a fancy for. I wonder now what Mr. Latchet 'ud say, if any other man in the congregation were to stare at you as 'e does, Sunday after Sunday? I'm sure it's as much as I can do to sit still sometimes, 'e makes me that mad!"

"Martha!" broke forth Tryphena.

"Well, 'e does!" affirmed Martha, stoutly—"an old yellow-faced feller like 'im, too. 'E ought to be ashamed of 'isself. I shall tell 'im so some day—you see if I don't."

"Oh, but Martha," reiterated Tryphena, in a tone of anguish, "you must not say such things—indeed and indeed you must not; you do not know how you hurt me. Why, if I thought other people talked like that, I should go wild—I should be ready to kill myself for pure shame. Cannot you see how shocking it would be?"

"Lord a mercy!" ejaculated Martha, coolly, "you're mighty thin-skinned. Mr. Latchet don't mind 'avin' his name coupled with yours, I'll bet. Not that it is coupled—or ever shall be, if I can 'elp it. It's a different sort of man to 'im that I should like to see your 'usband—very different!"

"I shall never have a husband at all," returned Tryphena, with mock melancholy, "if this sort of thing goes on, for I shall be dead long before anybody thinks of marrying me."

Martha smiled—smiled, and bit off a needleful of thread.

"All's well that ends well," observed she. "Do to-day's work to-day, I say, and to-morrow will do its own—but then I'm no scholar."

Tryphena sighed; scholarship, she thought, scarcely came into the question.

So Tuesday changed to Wednesday, and Wednesday to Thursday—morning to noon, and noon to afternoon. Aunt Rachel scrubbed and scoured, and fumed and fussed, as though on the spotlessness of the Grange floors, pots, pans, and copper tea-kettles depended not only the temporal but also the spiritual well-being of the coming guest—not merely the safety of his neck but of his soul. Jacob looked on and laughed. Tryphena neither looked on nor laughed, she had other things to do than that. The precise hour of Robert's arrival defied the nicest calculation. "I shall probably make my appearance about tea-time," he wrote, "but do not wait for me." "Just as though I shouldn't wait for him," observed Aunt Rachel, testily; "such senselessness."

By half-past three, however, as the sun went in, and over the cloudless sky spread that beautiful pale tint best seen in early winter, and like to the inside of a shell, moreover a sure token of dryness in the atmosphere, and quickly warmed to rose—everything needful was accomplished, even to the polishing of the hall-door knocker, and the setting forth of a nosegay on the spare room dressing-table. Tryphena was at liberty to change her frock when she pleased.

"You'd better put on your puce silk," remarked Aunt Rachel, as she untied her apron, "and you can wear a ribbon in your hair if you like. It is but fitting to make some little difference."

But Tryphena's face brightened not; to tell the truth, she was tired, having been up and at work since daybreak.

"No," answered she, quietly; "that would look very stupid, just as though I thought more of myself than of him. Besides, I've grown so since that puce silk was made, the skirt would be up to my knees. No, I shall have a good wash, and make myself tidy. There is no need for me to be anxious about my appearance."

"I suppose," observed Miss Fowke, "you think yourself quite pretty enough already?"

But Tryphena shook her head.

"Not I," smiled she, wearily, "I know my own face too well for that!"

Aunt Rachel unrolled her sleeves—what girls were made of was no secret to her, she flattered herself.

Still, despite this modest disavowal of all charm, it was plain, on a certain young woman's reappearance, her brief toilette being completed, that she had taken pains therewith—had even turned science to account in a manner alike daring and effective.

"So you've got on a ribbon, after all!" remarked Aunt Rachel, as, stiff with satinet and satisfaction, she rustled into the kitchen about an hour later—"and cherry-coloured.

Dear, dear! I don't know but what I rather like it, though," meditatively.

"I thought I looked so dull," replied Tryphena, bashfully, "in this gray dress, without a bit of trimming."

"It is a very good dress," was the dignified answer, "quite good enough for a girl of your age. I don't approve of young people being dressed out in silks and satins; besides, I told you when it was being made that you could have a row of velvet on the skirt if you chose."

"Yes, I know," said Tryphena—"I know you like me to be nice. That is why I took pains with my hair this afternoon, and put on my new shoes," exhibiting two slender sandalled little feet shod in black prunella; "but hark! what's that?"

"What's what?" ejaculated Aunt Rachel, blankly.

"Why, don't you hear a horse in the lane?—and"—looking out of the window—"there's father coming out of the foldyard—and ——"

But Aunt Rachel was already in the garden.

"You're right," called she, and seemed to run towards the gate.

Tryphena hurried to the door.

Yes, there he was, there in his great black hat and new brown riding-coat—the gray one hung in the cupboard in his bedroom, a ruined thing, despite all Aunt Rachel's spongings and pressings—there on Silvertail, who, dear old man, stretched out his neck and snuffed the air, as though he had a mind for some supper when it was convenient. And now the saddle was empty, and Mr. Valoynes, having stamped the frost out of his toes, was shaking hands with father and Aunt Rachel, and Aunt Rachel was talking and laughing, and looking round towards the house; and now, John having laid hold of Silvertail's bridle, they were all three coming up the path.

Tryphena's right cheek glowed as might a live coal.

"Come!" cried Miss Fowke, espying her upon the threshold, "where are your manners? Mr. Valoynes will think you're not glad to see him, if you're so backward in giving him a welcome; and I'm sure that wouldn't meet your wishes!"

"Indeed !" said Robert, prisoning her hand in his—a timidly proffered hand, and just a little tremulous, his deep dark eyes fed meanwhile with the meek beauty of her sweet small face—" really ?"

But she would not look up at him—she would only smile and say hurriedly :

" I hope that you are quite well, sir ?"

Cur non, Deo juvante.

END OF VOL. I.